ABERDEEN
CITY LIBRARIES
www.aberdeencity.gov.uk/libraries

WAGONS EAST!

The flint-eyed Texan was a man with a mission—get the wagon train across the treacherous prairies and mountains, deliver its cargo into the hands of the Confederacy. None of the homeward-bound pioneers knew that the contraband gold was hidden beneath the false floors of their Conestogas. No one guessed that the wagon master was a Rebel officer—a man who was going to win the war for the South single-handedly—or kill them all trying.

Lewis B. Patten wrote more than ninety Western novels in thirty years and three of them won Spur Awards from the Western Writers of America and the author himself the Golden Saddleman Award. Indeed, this highlights the most remarkable aspect of his work: not that there is so much of it, but that so much of it is so fine. Patten was born in Denver, Colorado, and served in the U.S. Navy 1933–1937. He was educated at the University of Denver during the war years and became an auditor for the Colorado Department of Revenue during the 1940s. It was in this period that he began contributing significantly to Western pulp magazines, fiction that was from the beginning fresh and unique and revealed Patten's lifelong concern with the sociological and psychological effects of group psychology on the frontier. He became a professional writer at the time of his first novel, *Massacre at White River* (1952). The dominant theme in much of his fiction is the notion of justice, and its opposite, injustice. In his first novel it has to do with exploitation of the Ute Indians, but as he matured as a writer he explored this theme with significant and poignant detail in small towns throughout the early West. Crimes, such as rape or lynching, were often at the centre of his stories. When the values embodied in these small towns are examined closely, they are found to be wanting. Conformity is always easier than taking a stand. Yet, in Patten's view of the American West, there is usually a man or a woman who refuses to conform. Among his finest titles, always a difficult choice, surely are *A Killing at Kiowa* (1972), *Ride a Crooked Trail* (1976), and his many fine contributions to Doubleday's Double D series, including *Villa's Rifles* (1977), *The Law at Cottonwood* (1978), and *Death Rides a Black Horse* (1978). His later books include *Tincup in the Storm Country* (1996), *Trail to Vicksburg* (1997), *Death Rides the Denver Stage* (1999), and *The Woman at Ox-Yoke* (2000).

WAGONS EAST!

Lewis B. Patten

GUNSMOKE

This hardback edition 2009
by BBC Audiobooks Ltd
by arrangement with
Golden West Literary Agency

ISBN 978 1 405 68163 6

British Library Cataloguing in Publication Data available.

Printed and bound in Great Britain by
CPI Antony Rowe, Chippenham, Wiltshire

chapter 1

It was an eerie world through which he rode, a world made up of swirling wisps of fog so thick that at times only the lush growth at the edge of the road was visible.

Below and to his left, angry surf pounded against the rock making a sustained and steady roar. And he was cold. All the way to his bones. After the baking, dry heat of the desert this dampness made him shiver violently, made him clench his jaws to keep his teeth from chattering.

Now and again he would hear the mournful wail of a foghorn, and another, answering the first, as two tall-masted ships sought to pass each other inside the fog-locked bay. And then, so suddenly that it took him completely by surprise, he was riding down a steep hill on a cobblestone street, and buildings were on both sides of him.

Lights materialized briefly out of the fog, disappearing almost immediately into it again. The horse, unused to cobblestone pavement, picked his way cautiously. A wariness not apparent before came over the man.

He was tall, this Vince MacIvers, and he rode in a deliberate and unaccustomed slouch. He was clad in a cape that covered him from neck to knees. His hat, spotted now with dust and mud and faded from the sun, had once been black.

He wore no beard, though his jaws showed a three-day growth of light stubble. Beneath a flickering street lamp he reined his horse to a halt and peered at the street sign. Oriented immediately, he turned right and continued for two more blocks before turning left.

He rode closer to the buildings now, trying to make out street numbers. He halted finally before a towering, three-story, brown-frame house, dismounted, tied his horse to the ornate cast-iron hitching post, and walked stiffly to the door.

5

Here, he pulled the cape back away from his right side, exposing the holstered, long-barreled revolver hanging there. He hesitated a moment, his face hidden by darkness and by fog. Then, decisively, he pounded on the door with his fist.

He waited for what seemed an interminable time. He knocked again, and this time there was an unmistakable rhythm about the way he knocked. The door opened.

The entry was dark, but he could see the shape of a man framed in it. Without speaking, he stepped inside.

His hand was close to the exposed grips of his revolver as he followed the man who had admitted him down a long hall and into a lighted room. There was a fire burning in the fireplace. MacIvers crossed the room and put his back to it.

The man he faced was squat and broad, with an outsize head that made him seem top-heavy. He was bearded and his eyes were blue and penetrating. MacIvers said, "There was a Stonewall just outside of town. I ate in the Lee of it. When I finished I rode into town and down a Longstreet. Your place wasn't hard to find because I have studied maps of San Francisco."

The other man's heavy face softened slightly and he turned his head. "All right. You three can come in."

Three men came into the room. All were bearded, roughly dressed, and armed. The squat man smiled faintly. "We take no chances." He crossed to MacIvers and put out his powerful hand. "I'm Brody. These three are Coulter, Abel, and Rossiter."

MacIvers said, "I'm Vince MacIvers," and took the powerful hand.

Brody gripped his hand briefly. "You know the plan?"

Coulter said harshly, "Wait a minute. How do we know ——"

Brody turned his massive head and stared at the man. "How do we know he's what he says he is? We don't. But we will know before we let him out of our sight." He turned back to MacIvers. "What is the plan, Mr. MacIvers?"

MacIvers said, "You've got five million in gold bullion. I'm to organize a wagon train and take it east. I'm to deliver it to the Confederacy as soon as possible."

"Ever taken a wagon train over either of the trails between here and Missouri?"

MacIvers shook his head.

"Then why the hell——"

MacIvers felt a stir of irritation. He was tired and hungry and had expected to be met with something more palatable than suspicion. He interrupted, "Mister, I'm a Texan. I'm no

6

stranger either to wagons or to rough country. Get me wagons, and I'll get the damn things through."

A faint smile appeared on Brody's mouth, but the eyes of the other three showed no softening. Brody said, "Good enough. Come on to the kitchen. I'll fix you something to eat, and then you can get some sleep."

Coulter said, "Brody, we ought to get his gun."

MacIvers shifted his glance to Coulter. He said irritably, "You get it, mister."

Brody chuckled. He said, "Yeah. You get it, Coulter."

"You think I can't?" Coulter took a forward step.

Brody said softly, "No shooting, now. We want no noise. Not with all that bullion hidden here."

The irritation in MacIvers was growing, fed by the anticipatory gleam in Coulter's eyes, by the speculative light in Brody's. Coulter, he understood, wanted him disarmed. But Brody— Brody just wanted to see how tough he was.

He waited, studying Coulter as the man advanced toward him warily.

Coulter was no taller than he, and his loose-fitting clothes tended to conceal his bulk. But MacIvers knew the man was at least ten pounds heavier than he.

Coulter, a loose-moving, raw-boned man, crossed to MacIvers. He stopped a yard away and said, "The gun, man. We need a whole man for the job we want done, not a cripple."

MacIvers smiled faintly, "And you think you're likely to cripple me?"

Coulter scowled. His eyes, a tawny, cold color, narrowed. Like a cat who has carefully stalked a bird and is ready for its final rush, he swung a bony fist.

It whistled past MacIvers' face as he jerked his head away. Then Coulter's body slammed against him and carried him back, against the fireplace, almost into it.

Pinned there momentarily, MacIvers felt Coulter's hand groping for his gun. His own weariness and irritation suddenly became anger, white-hot and unrestrained.

His knee came up savagely. Coulter grunted sharply with pain and doubled against MacIvers, whose fist chopped at the side of his hairy neck.

The man fell away, staggering, and MacIvers followed, swinging a long, hard right that slammed into Coulter's jaw.

The force of it sent Coulter crashing against a table, which overturned. But the impact steadied him. He stopped, and crouched, and turned his narrowed, tawny eyes toward MacIvers. His hand fumbled for something and came up holding a gleaming knife with a blade six inches long.

7

Brody roared, "Coulter! Put that thing away!"

Coulter didn't seem to hear. He grinned slightly at MacIvers and took a step toward him. Brody roared again, "Coulter!"

Coulter lunged, his arm making a wide, cutting sweep with the knife. MacIvers leaped back, feeling the tug as the blade cut the loose flap of his cape. He snatched off the cape and flung it over Coulter's head.

The man tried to pull it off. In that instant of fumbling, MacIvers seized the knife wrist with one hand, his elbow with the other, and brought the arm down violently against his rising knee.

He heard the bone snap, heard Coulter's sharp intake of breath. An instant later he heard the clatter of the knife falling to the floor. He released Coulter's arm and gave him a quick push with both hands.

Coulter staggered back, fighting for balance, and fell against the far wall with a crash. With his good hand he snatched the cape from his head. Awkwardly he fumbled for his gun. He got it out and tried to thumb the hammer back.

Brody kicked the gun out of his hand. He said, "Stupid! That's enough!"

Coulter was grunting softly with pain. He stared steadily at MacIvers, his eyes virulent. Brody said, "Get the son of a bitch out of here."

Abel and Rossiter crossed to Coulter and helped him to his feet. Once up, he shook them off impatiently, wincing with the pain the movement caused. He shuffled out of the room. The other two followed.

Brody turned his ponderous head and looked irritably at MacIvers. "That was a stupid thing to do. Now——"

MacIvers interrupted, "What do you think I should have done? Let him open me up like a deer?"

Brody studied him briefly. He shrugged.

"You said something about food. And sleep. I could use some of both."

"All right. Come on."

MacIvers retrieved his cape. Carrying it over his arm, he followed Brody from the room. They went along a long hall, through an empty room probably intended for a dining room, and into a kitchen beyond.

Brody stirred the fire in the stove and added wood. He went outside and returned with a piece of meat and a handful of potatoes. He put the meat in a pan and began to peel the potatoes.

The stove began to give off heat. MacIvers sat down and watched the squat man move around as efficiently as a woman would. He asked, "Have you got the wagons yet?"

"We have them. They're in an old livery barn not far from here."

"How——"

"They've been altered. We've had a carpenter build a false floor into each of them. The gold will be hidden there."

"And the people?"

Brody turned his head and glanced at him. "There are plenty in California who want to go home."

MacIvers nodded. He knew the chances of getting the gold to Missouri were poor. Yet he also knew with what difficulty the gold had been acquired—by armed raids on mines and stagecoaches and banks. Men had died for it, and more would die before it reached its destination.

He knew what he himself would do to see that it arrived. For an instant his expression was sober, his eyes narrowed and filled with memory.

He had volunteered for the Army of the Confederacy because he believed in a principle. He had left his ranch and had taken his wife to a neighbor's so that she would be safe while he was gone.

Only she hadn't been safe. She was dead, and so were the neighbors; both theirs and MacIvers' ranch buildings had been burned. Comanches had raided before MacIvers had been gone two months.

If he'd stayed, his wife might still be alive. His face hardened briefly.

He had nothing left. Only the captain's bars he wore when he was in uniform. Only the cause, and if the cause failed, it meant his wife had died in vain.

Five million dollars in gold might not save the faltering Confederacy. But it would help. MacIvers meant to see that it got through. No matter what he had to do. No matter who got hurt.

So far things had not gone well. He had crippled a man who should have been his ally. He had made an enemy who could be dangerous.

He was suddenly anxious to get on with it. As Brody put a plate in front of him, he said, "We'll forget the sleep until after I've seen the wagons."

Brody shrugged.

MacIvers said, "And I'll need some men. At least one or two who know what we're carrying."

Brody grinned ruefully at him. "I figured on giving you two. Coulter and Abel. Both of them want to enlist. Or say they do."

9

MacIvers finished eating and stood up. "Let's go look at the wagons."

Brody nodded. He opened the door, and MacIvers followed him into the foggy night.

chapter 2

They emerged at the rear of the tall house. In the distance, out of the shroud of fog, MacIvers could hear, faintly, the mournful squawl of foghorns in the bay. Other sounds were effectively muffled by the fog.

He followed Brody toward the alley, passing a stable, and Brody said, "Sounds like your horse has been watered and fed."

MacIvers didn't reply. In the darkness and fog, Brody sometimes all but disappeared in front of him.

He had traveled more than three thousand miles through mostly hostile country, but until now he had not experienced the sense of being surrounded by enemies he was feeling now. And he knew the feeling would increase. He must travel back, through Union territory, leading a train of wagons in which five million dollars in gold had been concealed.

They'd be overloaded. Each wagon must carry close to a ton of gold in addition to its normal load. The trail was unfamiliar. If he was caught, if the gold was discovered, he would be hanged.

He bumped into Brody, who had halted suddenly. Brody unlocked a padlock and MacIvers followed him into a huge livery barn, even darker than the night outside.

Brody struck a match, found a lantern, and lighted it. He led MacIvers along a line of large canvas-covered wagons. Brody said, "They're the best to be found. They've been gone over from top to bottom and they're sound."

"Have you organized the train?"

"It is being done."

MacIvers counted the wagons. There were eight in all. He took the lantern from Brody and inspected one briefly.

He returned the lantern. "How much has to be done on the gold compartments?"

"They're finished. The gold can be loaded by dawn, and by sunup the false floors can be in place."

MacIvers took the lantern again and climbed up into one of the wagons. He knelt and examined the work that had been done on the floor.

Whoever had done it was good. The compartment was no deeper than necessary to hold the bars of bullion. It could be covered with a false floor which had already been cut from weathered boards, apparently taken from other wagons. MacIvers picked one of them up and examined it in the lantern light. Even the ends appeared to be old and weathered. Unless someone started measuring, the compartment would never be found.

He climbed down out of the wagon, handed the lantern back to Brody, and asked, "Is the train going to be formed right here?"

Brody shook his head. "The wagons will be driven to a rendezvous point ten miles south of town. The families that are to go will meet you there. You'll be given a list of the amount each is to pay. And you'll be given some specie. Use what you need of the money along the way. Turn over the rest, along with the bullion, when you reach your destination."

MacIvers nodded. Other questions were buzzing in his head, but he knew that time would answer them. One question needed an answer, though, and now. He said, "How many of you are there? How many know your plans?"

Brody frowned. "Myself. The carpenter. Abel and Coulter and Rossiter. Two others who are organizing the train, Hawkins and Dupree. Yourself. That's eight in all."

It was too many, but MacIvers knew it could not be helped. He would just have to hope that everybody concerned kept still.

Brody said, "Come on, then, if you're satisfied."

He led MacIvers to the rear of the livery barn. He nudged a man sleeping on a pile of hay. The man sat up, startled, then began to rub his eyes.

Brody said, "MacIvers, this is Carmichael, the carpenter."

Carmichael was a slight, bearded man, wearing nothing but red-flannel underwear and socks. He stuck out a hand, scratching himself with the other. He grinned. "Glad to see you, cap'n."

"Don't call me captain."

"Sorry. You looked at my work? What do you think of it? Ever see new-cut boards look that old before? It's done with

12

paint. The colors got to match just right or the whole thing's wrong."

"How long since they were painted?" He tried to remember if he had smelled paint and decided that he had.

Carmichael chuckled. "We thought of that too, cap'n. So we painted all the wagon bows."

Brody interrupted, "MacIvers, stay here and sleep. Carmichael, I'll be back with the gold in a couple of hours. I want those floors in place over it by sunup."

"You get the gold here, Mr. Brody, and I'll get the boards in place."

Carrying the lantern, Brody walked toward the front of the barn. Carmichael lighted another lantern and began to dress. "Go to sleep, cap'n."

MacIvers sat down on the pile of hay. He shifted his revolver so that it was exposed to his hand. He laid back and closed his eyes.

Everything seemed to be going all right, he thought. The work was done, and by sunup the gold would be in place. The wagons would move out, each driven separately to the rendezvous point. The train would be formed by nightfall, ready to start the following day.

Perhaps, he thought, it was all too smooth. Perhaps that was why this feeling of uneasiness troubled him. Or perhaps it was Abel and Coulter and Rossiter that bothered him. He didn't like them, and he didn't trust them.

Brody, however, had impressed him as a man driven by his convictions. Brody would have been the man behind the idea of transporting gold to the Confederacy, which desperately needed it to bolster its failing credit with foreign powers. Brody would have been ruthless enough and shrewd enough to plan and carry out the raids that had resulted in obtaining it. Brody's mind had undoubtedly conceived the wagon train as being the safest way of getting it to the South.

The man as a patriot, selfless and dedicated. The others. . . .

MacIvers frowned. A man became used to judging the character of other men when he commanded a company of cavalry. And he had liked not one of the three he'd met.

He dozed, but wakened at each small noise within the enormous barn. He found himself wishing he had not broken Coulter's arm. He'd need the man. He'd need all the help he could get.

Near dawn, he was wakened by voices and by the racket of two freight wagons being driven into the livery barn. He got up and walked to the front of the barn.

Brody and Abel and Rossiter were there. They began immediately to unload the bars. Abel and Rossiter passed them down to Brody and MacIvers, who loaded them into the other wagons. Though small, the bars were exceedingly heavy. MacIvers began to sweat heavily with exertion.

Brody counted the bars into each wagon, and when one was fully loaded, Carmichael bolted the false floorboards in place. The sun came up, filtering through the dirty windows of the barn.

An hour after sunup, the job was done. Abel and Rossiter backed the freight wagons out of the way and unhitched the teams. They led them into the corral, in which there were fifty or sixty mules.

Working together now, they caught mules, six for each wagon, harnessed them, and hitched up one wagon after another. Two more men arrived. Rossiter drove the first wagon and disappeared into the thinning morning fog. Abel took the second. Hawkins and Dupree, the new arrivals, took the third and fourth.

Coulter arrived as the fourth was driving away. Brody growled, "We haven't got enough men. Coulter can't drive six mules with a broken arm. One of us will have to come back. Coulter can get your saddle horse. You can trail him along behind."

He gave MacIvers swift directions for reaching the rendezvous. MacIvers went out into the corral to catch mules for the wagon he was to drive. Brody accompanied him.

They caught six mules, three each, and lead them back toward the barn. Just inside the door, MacIvers stopped.

Carmichael lay curled up on the floor, a knife protruding from his belly. Coulter stood over him.

Brody growled, "Oh, for God's sake! What's happened now?"

Coulter turned, scowling. "The son of a bitch was tryin' to blackmail me. Said one bar wouldn't be missed, and if we figured he was going to keep still, we'd better give it to him."

Brody cursed savagely. "Now we're two men short. MacIvers, you bring someone else back with you. Coulter, go get MacIvers' saddle horse. I'll get rid of Carmichael."

Coulter stooped and awkwardly, with his left hand, withdrew his knife. He wiped the bloody blade unconcernedly on Carmichael's coat. He straightened, glanced sullenly at Brody, then left the barn to get MacIvers' horse.

MacIvers began to harness the mules. Brody helped. Coulter returned by the time they had finished leading the saddle horse. He tied it behind the wagon and climbed awkwardly to the seat.

MacIvers drove out. He didn't believe Coulter's story that

Carmichael had tried to blackmail him. Yet Brody had apparently accepted it.

The morning was cool and damp, but the fog had cleared away. From this high vantage point MacIvers could see the bay, vast and mostly empty. He could see the cluster of ships docked below, their masts like a forest bare of leaves.

It was early and there was not much traffic on the streets. No one paid any attention to them, and within half an hour, MacIvers had left the town, dropped down into a valley, and lost view of the bay and the sea beyond.

He followed the directions Brody had given him. Beside him, Coulter sat in silence, occasionally grunting softly with pain as he shifted position on the seat. MacIvers noted that his arm had been splinted and bandaged and was now carried in a white-cotton sling.

He turned his head and stared back at the huge wagon. It was a smaller version of the old-time Conestoga wagon, but it was still large for the rugged trip east. The bed was fourteen feet long, four and a half feet wide, and the sides were five and a half feet high. The rear wheels were almost as tall as MacIvers' six feet, and the spindles were three inches in diameter.

He wondered if the size of the wagons would arouse suspicion, since it would be obvious to almost anyone that the emigrants' possessions constituted a very light load for them.

Nothing had been said about spare mules, but MacIvers knew they'd need close to fifty. Perhaps, he thought, the emigrants would furnish them. Or perhaps, once the wagons were at the rendezvous, some of the men would return for them.

The miles passed slowly. Coulter maintained his sullen silence. On a steep grade, MacIvers tried the ratchet brake and noted with satisfaction that the wagon ground to a halt. He released the brake sufficiently to let the wagon roll down the grade.

Following Brody's directions, he left the road, traveled through a dense thicket of brush, and emerged into a clearing surrounded by tall trees. He pulled his wagon up beside the other four, locked the brake, and climbed down.

The others, and perhaps a dozen people strange to him, were grouped around a fire. He crossed to them, and Rossiter shouted, "Here's your wagon master, folks. Vince MacIvers. He's going to take you east."

MacIvers acknowledged the introduction, studying the people one by one. He glanced beyond them at the collection of carts and broken-down wagons which had brought them and their possessions to the rendezvous.

He was aware that they were sizing him up, making an estimate of him, just as he was making one of them. He turned his head and looked at Hawkins, a graying man in his early fifties. "You'll have to go back with me. Brody is short of drivers."

"I'll get a horse."

MacIvers got his own horse, which was tied behind the wagon. He mounted, joined Hawkins, and the two rode out again, heading west. Out of the hearing of the others, Mac-Ivers said, "Coulter can't drive because of his broken arm. And he stuck a knife in Carmichael after you had left."

"For God's sake, why?"

"He claimed Carmichael wanted a bar of gold to keep him quiet."

"I don't believe that."

"Neither do I."

Hawkins glanced at him. "If I was you, I'd watch Coulter pretty close. Especially when you get near the end of the trip."

MacIvers nodded. He'd watch Coulter all the way, not just at the end of the trip.

He wondered if, among the emigrants, there would be anyone he could trust. He doubted it. Certainly he could trust no one with his knowledge of the purpose of the journey, or the cargo carried by the wagons. If he ever delivered the gold to the Confederacy it would be a miracle.

Then he thought of his ranch in Texas, its house and buildings burned to the ground. He thought of his wife, now dead, and wondered what she had been forced to endure before she died.

His face twisted with the memory. And his eyes turned hard. He would do whatever had to be done to make the journey succeed. He would kill Coulter—and Abel, too—if it was necessary.

chapter 3

The return trip was made without incident. Neither Mac-Ivers nor Hawkins mentioned Carmichael, and neither did Brody. MacIvers guessed that Brody had buried him beneath the livery-stable floor, for he was still sweating heavily.

Hawkins drove out first, followed by MacIvers. Brody brought up the rear. The streets were busy now, but no one more than glanced at them.

It was midafternoon by the time they reached the rendezvous. MacIvers noted immediately that extra mules had been provided. There were now close to a hundred rope-corralled at one side of the clearing.

Hawkins and Brody began to unhitch the teams. MacIvers crossed to the crowd of emigrants, talking and swapping stories. He said, "I'd like to meet you individually. Come to my wagon in family groups, and I'll assign wagons to you and give you numbers to be painted on them."

He returned to his wagon. He lowered the endgate. Brody brought him a cashbox and a board with several sheets of paper attached. There was a list of names on the top sheet, and beside the names were the amounts paid and the amounts still due.

The first name on the list was Wilcox. MacIvers called, "The Wilcox family first."

A man and woman detached themselves timidly from the group and approached. The man was middle-aged and partly bald. He carried his hat in his two hands in front of him.

He nodded at MacIvers and smiled hesitantly. "Ned Wilcox, cap'n. My wife Molly."

"No children, Mr. Wilcox?"

Ned Wilcox glanced quickly at his wife. Then he said,

17

"We had four, cap'n. We lost every one of them—the last one just two months ago from lung fever. Three we lost on the trail coming west. We just figure there ain't nothin' to keep us here now. It was kind of for the kids we came in the first place. We're goin' home."

"Where's home, Mr. Wilcox?"

"Illinois. We ain't got a farm no more. Sold it when we came west. I reckon we'll just live in town till I get a stake together again."

The man looked lean and strong. And there was a steadiness in his eyes, a firmness about his mouth. MacIvers nodded. "Forty-seven dollars is what you still owe, Mr. Wilcox. Take that wagon over there. Paint a one on the side."

He watched the pair walk away, the woman staying close beside her husband. As they reached their wagon, he put a hand on her shoulder and smiled at her.

He looked at the second name on the list. It was Peebles. He called, "Mr. Peebles."

Another man and woman detached themselves from the group. The man was stringy and sharp-eyed, the woman big, rawboned, and two inches taller than he. Peebles stuck out his hand after wiping it on the leg of his pants. He was not very clean and needed both a shave and a haircut. He said in a nasal, diffident voice, "Lew Peebles, wagon master. My wife Charity."

"Children?"

"No, sir. The Lord ain't seen fit to bless us with 'em. We got no one to help us now we're gettin' old. Not that I'm complainin', you understand. It's just that—"

MacIvers said, "You still owe thirty dollars. Take that wagon next to Ned Wilcox and paint an eight on it."

Peebles stared at him a moment, then handed him some worn bills, and shuffled away, followed by his wife.

MacIvers called, "Effinger."

Jess Effinger was a big, black-haired man with a full black beard. He was dressed in a suit and looked like a preacher. His eyes held those of MacIvers steadily as he approached, followed by his wife and three children.

He put out a strong hand, the back of which was thickly covered with hair. His grip was strong. His voice had a sharp, clipped, Yankee twang. "Jess Effinger, Mr. MacIvers. My wife Mary. And Lucy, Mark, and Luke."

The girl was pretty and about sixteen years old. She looked up at MacIvers, flushed, then looked at the ground. Mark, about nine, grinned at MacIvers. The other boy, about seven, hid behind his mother's skirt.

MacIvers said, "You're paid up, Mr. Effinger. Take that wagon next to Peebles and paint a two on it."

Effinger looked at him sharply. "You talk like a Southerner, Mr. MacIvers. I——"

MacIvers interrupted quickly, "The war's in the East, Mr. Effinger. All we're concerned with is getting these wagons there. It'll be best all around if you keep your politics to yourself."

"That I can't promise to do, sir. I feel strongly about human beings held in bondage."

MacIvers shrugged. "Make trouble, sir, and I'll hold you accountable. We'll have no undersized war between the states going on in this wagon train."

"Don't you mean war of rebellion, sir?"

"I meant what I said. I'm telling you to keep still about the war. If you can't do that, you can stay behind."

Mrs. Effinger murmured something to her husband. He flushed slightly, then nodded. "You're the wagon master, Mr. MacIvers."

There were only six people left at the fire. Two of these were young women under thirty. Another was a middle-aged man, handsome and self-assured. The other three appeared to be a family group.

MacIvers looked questioningly at Brody. Brody said softly, "The only family left is the Busbys. The two women were going to share a wagon, but that was before the O'Hare family changed their minds about going. Now they'll each have to take a wagon."

MacIvers nodded. He called Busby.

The three MacIvers had guessed composed a family group detached themselves from the others and approached. The woman's features were pinched and sharp. The man was unshaven and as dirty as Peebles. The boy, who appeared to be about seventeen, followed behind them, meeting MacIvers' glance almost defiantly.

MacIvers said, "You still owe sixty dollars."

Busby mumbled, "That's what I want to talk to you about. We ain't got it. We had some tough luck. Seems like——"

MacIvers said, "You and your boy can work it out. Driving for those two women who will be traveling alone."

A gleam that was almost triumphant appeared in Busby's eyes. He glanced aside at his wife, his expression saying, "Didn't I tell you I could put it over?"

MacIvers said, "Your wagon will be number six."

"Sure, cap'n." There was a drawl to Busby's voice that reminded MacIvers of a man who had been in his company.

19

He asked, "You from Tennessee, Mr. Busby?"

"We sure are, cap'n. We sure are. My boy, John, wants to enlist, but I tell him it ain't right for him to leave us now—just when he can be some help to us."

MacIvers watched them walk away. Busby might be from the South, but he knew he could expect little support from this man if trouble came.

He called, "Sally Bullock."

One of the women came toward him. She was yellow-haired and pretty, dressed in a close-fitting gown of dark-colored wool. Her eyes were coolly appraising.

He said, "You'll have to take a wagon by yourself, Miss Bullock. But you'll have help driving."

"Thank you, Mr. MacIvers." Her eyes held his steadily, and her voice was throaty, almost hoarse.

He said, "Your wagon will be number three. You'll be behind Mr. Effinger."

"Thank you." She turned and walked away, hips swaying slightly as she walked.

Brody murmured, "Saloon girl."

MacIvers nodded. His impression of the girl had been that she was capable. Yet something about her bothered him. He frowned and decided that it was the firmness in her eyes and mouth—as if she had a purpose stronger than merely getting from one part of the country to another.

He glanced at the other woman, waiting by the fire. He called, "Mrs. Cory."

The woman came toward him. Brody said softly, "She's a widow. Her husband was killed at Bull Run."

She put out a hand and MacIvers took it briefly. He said, "Your wagon will be number five. Behind mine. You'll have help driving."

She was dark-haired, dressed in a fresh gingham gown. In some vague way she reminded him of his wife. She asked, "Why don't you just leave one of the wagons behind? Miss Bullock and I could share one."

He said, "Things happen on the trail, Mrs. Cory. Wagons get wrecked. It will be just as well if we have a spare."

The explanation sounded lame, even to MacIvers. But she seemed to accept it. She walked toward one of the empty wagons. MacIvers called, "Locke."

The middle-aged man left the fire, smiling affably. Brody muttered, "This one deals in women, Mr. MacIvers. He brings 'em west after telling them husbands are waiting for them. Only there aren't any husbands waiting. All that's waiting are the saloons. He's got a way with 'em, though. He's heading back east for another load."

MacIvers stared at Locke. The man stuck out a fleshy hand. "Jack Locke, Mr. MacIvers. Jacklock, they call me."

MacIvers said, "You owe sixty dollars, Mr. Locke. And your wagon will be number seven. Behind the Busbys."

Jacklock walked away after handing MacIvers three twenty-dollar gold pieces.

MacIvers handed the list to Brody. He said shortly, "We're undermanned. We're badly undermanned."

Brody stared at him thoughtfully. "They'll shape up once you're on the trail."

"Maybe."

Brody said, "They're the best I could get for you, MacIvers. They're all I could get."

"I thought you said plenty of families wanted to go home."

Brody grinned sheepishly. "Maybe I exaggerated a little. Maybe I didn't want to tell you right then what you'd have to work with."

"I could still refuse. There's not much chance of getting there with a crew like this."

"But you won't refuse, Mr. MacIvers."

MacIvers grinned briefly. "No, I guess not." He wished again that he hadn't broken Coulter's arm.

He watched them work at loading their possessions. It was true, of course, that none of them were green. All had come west by wagon train.

But there were so few. He counted the men. Wilcox. Peebles. Effinger. Jacklock, Busby, and Busby's son. Coulter, Abel, and himself. Nine men. It wasn't enough to take eight wagons east. They needed twice that many.

Yet he realized, too, that being so seriously undermanned had its advantages. No Union cavalry commander would suspect anyone of being foolish enough to move gold with a crew like this.

He glanced at Brody. "Five million is a lot of gold. Someone in San Francisco must suspect what's going on. They probably have an idea it's for the South. They may be searching every wagon train."

Brody's glance sharpened. He nodded. "You can count on being searched before you've gone fifty miles. But that's where this bunch of sorry pilgrims will pay off. Nobody will suspect this train when they see that bunch."

MacIvers shrugged fatalistically.

Jacklock was helping Mrs. Cory load her things. She seemed grateful for the help. Hawkins and Dupree drove a cart up beside MacIvers' wagon and began to toss things into it: bedding, cases of canned and dried food, ammunition, cooking utensils, axes, shovels, and great coils of heavy rope. MacIvers

21

climbed into the wagon and began to load them so that they wouldn't shift.

Then came extra harness, extra halters for the mules. For a while he forgot his doubts. Whatever happened, he was committed to taking the wagon train east.

As soon as he had the load stowed properly, he climbed down. Brody shook his hand. "We'll get going now. Good luck."

MacIvers grinned unconvincingly and watched Brody, Hawkins, and Dupree ride away.

He wasn't the only Southerner trying to do a job with less than the proper tools, he thought. Few Confederate commanders had enough of anything—food, guns, ammunition, clothing, or medical supplies.

But if he reached there with the gold, that would be changed. Or partly changed. Five million would buy a lot of guns. Perhaps enough to turn the tide.

The wagons were loaded. Fires had been built and the air was filled with cooking smells. Coulter and Abel were eating with Sally Bullock, and both were grinning at her like fools. Jack Locke was eating with Mrs. Cory.

She looked up and saw him standing there. She called, "Mr. MacIvers, have you eaten yet?"

He shook his head and walked toward her. Jacklock scowled at him. He accepted a plate from Mrs. Cory and squatted beside the fire to eat. He stared soberly into the flames.

The journey east would be hazardous. The wagons were too heavy, too big for the mountains they had to cross. The plains tribes were hostile, and he could expect little protection from the undermanned frontier garrisons. The train itself was undermanned.

There would be quarreling among the members of the group. Not only because of their opposing views on slavery, but also because two pretty single women were along.

He finished eating and stood up. He thanked Mrs. Cory and walked away. These wagons and these people were what he had, and all he had. He would make them do and would deliver the gold to the Confederacy. If he failed, the guilt he already felt over the death of his wife would become intolerable.

chapter 4

MacIvers was up half an hour before dawn. He stretched, then rolled up his blankets and tossed them into the wagon. Coulter and Abel were sleeping underneath the wagon.

He yelled, "Roll out! Let's get going!"

Across the clearing there was the stir of awakening. After several minutes, freshly kindled fires winked.

Coulter cursed steadily at his own awkwardness as he rolled up his blankets and stowed them in the wagon, but he did not ask for help.

Abel asked, "Which route are we going to take?"

"Northern. We won't try to herd the mules until we get away from the settlements, so tell everyone to catch an extra six or seven and tie them behind their wagons."

Abel walked away, a quick-moving, wiry man whose face was as impassive as though it were carved from wood. MacIvers stirred the embers of last night's fire and added wood. It smoked furiously for several minutes before it burst into flame.

Coulter growled, "You're a damn fool if you take the northern route. You'll have Union cavalry on your tail every inch of the way."

"Maybe. And maybe they'll figure nobody with any sense would take the northern trail unless they had nothing to hide."

"You're wrong. Brody——"

"Brody's job is done. This part of the job is mine. We're going to take the northern trail. Now shut up and go catch some mules."

Coulter shuffled away into the darkness, grumbling. Abel returned and began to heat water for coffee. He found bacon

23

and put it on to cook. He stirred up some biscuits, put them in a Dutch oven, and set it on the fire.

MacIvers said, "We'll circle around the bay, cross the San Joaquin River, and follow the Sacramento to Sacramento. We'll head up over Donner Pass and follow the Truckee down the other side. You ever been over that route?"

Abel looked up in the graying light. "Yeah. I been over it, and it's a son of a bitch. You'll break these wagons apart on the rocks. You'll need twelve mules to a wagon for some of the grades. You'll have to lower 'em down the other side by snubbin' ropes to trees. Best you go south to the Gila and across to Albuquerque."

"And what'll we do for water while we're traveling that southern route? I came that way. This time of year the rivers are dry, and so are the tanks."

"I'll find water when we need it. I been over that trail twice."

MacIvers stared at Abel's face. The man tried to meet his glance steadily and failed. A faint flush touched his unshaven cheeks. MacIvers said, "You and Coulter wouldn't be planning to take some of this bullion to Mexico would you?"

"That's a hell of a thing to say. We risked our necks to help Brody get it together."

MacIvers said, "All right. But we'll go the northern route."

The clearing was now filled with shouting and cursing, with the sound of plunging hoofs and the jangling of harness rings and tug chains. MacIvers gulped a couple of biscuits and several chunks of half-raw bacon. He swallowed a cup of coffee, then helped Coulter harness up the mules. He saddled his horse, mounted, and rode through the camp, sometimes dismounting to help, sometimes offering a word of advice.

It seemed impossible that order could come out of so much confusion, but as the sun came up, Wilcox drove the lead wagon out, to be followed by Effinger, Sally Bullock, Abel and Coulter and Mrs. Cory in number five. The others took their places and the train moved out of clearing, leaving a rubble of discarded articles, broken-down carts and wagons, and one dead mule that had broken a leg and had had to be shot.

MacIvers trotted his horse to the head of the column and rode beside Wilcox, who was driving. Wilcox' wife sat beside him, holding up a hand to shield her eyes from the rising sun.

MacIvers called, "How did you come west, Mr. Wilcox?"

"Same way we're goin' back, I'd say. Sacramento. Donner Pass. Salt Lake City. It's a rough one, Mr. MacIvers, but we got good wagons and plenty of mules."

24

MacIvers nodded.

Wilcox stared at him for several moments. "These wagons are heavy," he yelled. "They handle like they had an extra ton of weight in 'em."

"More iron than most, I guess. So they can take the mountains without breaking up." He watched Wilcox as he spoke, and was relieved that the man seemed to accept the explanation. He let his horse fall back, troubled that the question of weight had come up so soon.

They'd be searched, Brody had said, before they had gone fifty miles. He hoped neither Wilcox nor any of the others would mention weight while they were being searched. The authorities were undoubtedly watching for this missing gold and must have a pretty good idea as to how much of it there was.

He glanced up at Effinger as the man's wagon came abreast. "Everything all right?"

Effinger glanced at him briefly, frowning slightly. He nodded. MacIvers dropped back, abreast of Sally Bullock's wagon.

She was driving with the sleeves of her dress rolled up above her elbows. Her arms were brown and strong. She grinned at him and lowered her head to brush back a wisp of hair with her wrist. She'd need help later but she didn't need it now. He let his horse drop back until he was abreast of Mrs. Cory.

"Morning, Mrs. Cory. Need any help?" The way she turned her head reminded him of the way his wife had turned hers when he spoke to her. She shook her head and smiled, then shouted over the noise of the rumbling wagon, "My name's Donna, Mr. MacIvers."

He nodded, grinning at her. "When you need help, just ask for it. We've got several extra men."

He touched his heels to his horse's sides and galloped ahead to the front of the train.

Following narrow, steep roads built by gold seekers a dozen years before, they wound through the green and wooded hills surrounding San Francisco bay and at dusk camped at the bank of the San Joaquin River. A ferry crossed here, and MacIvers rode down to dicker with the ferryman. After several minutes of good-natured haggling, they settled on a price of two dollars a wagon.

Cookfires were winking beside the wagons when MacIvers returned. The women were cooking, and the men were gathered in a group close by. MacIvers heard their raised and angry voices even before he reached them. As he dismounted, Jess Effinger roared, "Slavery is a sin against God. And any man who keeps slaves is headed straight for hell!"

25

MacIvers strode to the man. "I told you to keep your politics to yourself!"

Effinger's face was flushed. His eyes narrowed as he shouted. "I'm not talking politics. I'm talking religion now."

"Then keep your religion to yourself. Some of these people are from the South. They can believe whatever they want to believe—and you can, too, as long as you keep still about it. Now break it up and go eat!"

Effinger glared at him. "I know your sympathies, sir."

"Damn it, my sympathies have got nothing to do with it. We've got mountains ahead, and deserts, and hostile tribes. We'll never reach the Missouri if we bicker and quarrel about slavery all the way. Now shut up, or unload your wagon right here and stay. Do I make myself clear?"

Effinger continued to scowl. But at last his furious stare shifted and he grumbled something under his breath. He turned and marched away, his back straight and eloquent of righteous indignation.

MacIvers looked at the others angrily. "Someone's been needling him. If I catch anybody at it, I'll leave him high and dry wherever it happens to be."

None of them would meet his glance. He walked to the wagon he shared with Abel and Coulter.

Coulter was whetting his knife, awkwardly holding the stone with his right hand. Abel was stirring a huge pot of beans. He said, "Look over there," pointing across the river.

MacIvers glanced in the direction he was pointing. There were more cookfires across the river, and in their light he could make out Union troopers moving back and forth.

The search Brody had warned him about would take place either tonight or in the morning. He stared at Abel, whose face was as wooden as it usually was. Abel wouldn't give anything away, he thought. He glanced at Coulter. There was a jerkiness about the way Coulter's knife moved on the stone.

MacIvers said, "They won't find anything. You both know how well the work was done. The only thing that might give us away is how we act when they begin to search. Act scared and they'll know damned well something's wrong."

Abel grunted, "He's right, Hugh. They're not going to find anything. How the hell could they?"

Coulter looked up. His eyes smoldered as he stared at MacIvers. But he didn't speak.

MacIvers left them and crossed the clearing. There was an uneasy feeling in his stomach. For an instant he wished he was back in Virginia.

That kind of war he understood. This kind— He didn't like his feeling of helplessness.

26

He heard Donna Cory's muffled voice call, "Mr. MacIvers!"

He turned in time to see Locke release her and step away. He felt a rising irritation. He walked to the two and said curtly, "Mr. Locke, get back to your own wagon."

Locke's face was flushed. Without speaking, he turned and walked into the darkness.

Donna Cory said, "I'm sorry, Mr. MacIvers. I know you must have troubles enough."

He shrugged, his irritation fading. He could see that she was tired and said, "Tomorrow I'll get Busby's boy to drive for you."

"Thank you." She hesitated a moment, then said softly, "Your voice sounds as if you were from the South, Mr. Mac-Ivers."

"Texas."

"How does it happen that you aren't——"

"With the Confederate army?" He hesitated for an instant. If he admitted to having been in the Confederate army, it would weaken his authority, particularly with Effinger. He said, "My wife was from the North, ma'am. Out of consideration for her——" He stopped, unused to lies and not wanting to go on.

There was immediate sympathy in her voice. "You say was. Is she——"

"She's dead. Comanches."

He wondered, suddenly, what this woman would say if he told her he had been at Bull Run, where her husband had been killed. He said coldly, "Good evening, Mrs. Cory," turned his back, and walked away.

It was the first time he had mentioned his wife's death to anyone. He discovered that he was angry and upset. He stopped at the river's edge and stared across at the cavalry troop's fires on the other side. He hoped Wilcox would keep still about how heavy the wagons were. He hoped Coulter. . . .

Impatient with himself, he returned to his wagon and helped himself to a plate of beans.

Some of the travelers were already turning in. The camp grew quiet gradually. Tomorrow, he thought, he'd detail a man or two to drive the extra mules behind the wagon train. It had been impossible for them to graze today. Tomorrow. . . .

He rummaged in the wagon until he found his blankets, then wrapped himself in them, and laid down beside the wagon to sleep.

27

chapter 5

In the morning MacIvers awoke to the brassy notes of the bugle, and for a fleeting instant he thought he was back with his unit in Virginia. Then he opened his eyes and remembered the wagon train, the gold, and the waiting troop of Union cavalry across the San Joaquin River.

He rolled out immediately, rubbed his whiskered face, rolled up his blankets, and tossed them into the wagon bed. He was dirty and unshaven, looking much more like a wagon master than a Confederate captain of cavalry, which was what he wanted now. He walked to the river, splashed water on his face, crammed on his hat, and turned toward the waking camp.

Women were taking in laundry, hastily washed and hung out the night before. Others were building fires, warming up beans and coffee left over from the evening meal.

Men were catching mules and harnessing. Again the bugle's clear notes came across the water, but MacIvers didn't glance that way again.

He walked to the rope corral where the mules were held, caught his horse, and led him to his wagon. He saddled, helped Abel harness up, then mounted and sat his saddle, surveying the camp.

At least it was better, he thought, than bringing a wagon train west. These people had all spent many a day on the trail and each knew what was expected of him, and when.

When all seemed ready, MacIvers bawled, "Last wagon first today," and watched Peebles drive his wagon toward the ferry, waiting at the river's edge.

He walked his horse that way, watching closely as Peebles drove onto the ferry. It settled in the water.

Following, he rode onto the ferry, quieting the prancing

28

animal with an inflexibly tight rein. He dismounted immediately as the ferryman chocked the wagon's wheels and closed the barrier behind. Peebles locked the ratchet brake.

The ferry inched out across the river. Staring ahead, MacIvers saw the cavalry, mounted, drawn up in line, waiting silently.

As soon as the ferry touched land, as soon as the barrier came down, he swung to his horse and rode toward them.

A lieutenant was in charge. His hat brim was pushed up in front and he wore a long cavalry-style moustache and clipped beard. He saluted, and MacIvers' hand twitched as he nearly returned the salute. He felt himself break out in a clammy sweat. That was something he had forgotten to be on guard against. A snappy return salute would have ruined everything.

Behind him he heard Peebles' whining voice cursing his teams, heard the creaking of the wagon as it rolled off the ferry. Peebles' whip cracked and the teams lunged up the slope.

The lieutenant, about MacIvers' age and obviously no newcomer to the service, said, "Heavy wagons, sir, for the mountain trails." He rode forward, removed the gauntlet from his right hand, and extended it.

MacIvers gripped it briefly. He said, "Vince MacIvers, lieutenant."

"Charles Foster. I'll have to search your wagons, Mr. MacIvers. I've orders to search every train that takes this road."

"Search? For what?"

The lieutenant peered at him, his eyes narrowed against the rising sun. He said cryptically, "Contraband." And he added, "You sound like a Texan, sir. Am I guessing right?"

MacIvers felt his stomach muscles tightening. He said, "You are." He turned his head and yelled, "Peebles!"

Peebles glanced at him and MacIvers beckoned. The wagon approached, mules leaning against the traces to pull it up the grade. Reaching fairly level ground, Peebles halted. MacIvers said, "The lieutenant wants to search. Let him look at anything he wants to see." He turned and glanced at Lieutenant Foster questioningly. "Is that all, lieutenant?"

"That's all, mister, for now."

MacIvers nodded. He rode his horse back to the ferry, dismounted, and led him onto it. The barrier went down and the ferry started back across.

MacIvers resisted the compulsion to look around. Nothing he could do now would alter the course of the search. The lieutenant and his men would poke around through Peebles' belongings until they were satisfied. They'd either find the hidden compartment or they would not.

He glanced at the ferryman, a giant of a man about sixty, heavily bearded and dark as any Comanche he had ever seen. "They search every wagon that comes along?"

"Yep." The man's voice was deep and cracked. "Lookin' fer bullion. There's been a heap of it stole in the last six months and nobody's figgered out where it went."

MacIvers glanced around. One cavalryman was under Peebles' wagon looking up. Another was peering into the water keg. Still another was tossing Peebles' belongings out onto the ground. Mrs. Peebles stood, hands on hips, lashing the lieutenant with her tongue.

In spite of the tension he was feeling, MacIvers grinned. Even from here the lieutenant's discomfort was obvious. The ferryman grunted, "She's sure givin' him hell, ain't she?"

"Looks like it. I expect he's thinking this is a hell of a way to fight a war."

When the ferry reached the other side, he mounted and rode off onto solid ground. The first wagon would be searched more diligently than any of the others, he thought.

Wilcox' wagon rumbled down the slope and onto the ferry. The barriers came up and the ferry moved out into the stream. Effinger drove his wagon toward the ferry, and as it passed, Lucy, whose face was peering out behind, smiled at MacIvers shyly. As the wagon passed that of the Busbys, her smile faded and she flushed. She quickly withdrew her head. John Busby was watching her from the seat beside his father.

MacIvers called, "Drive for Mrs. Cory this morning."

The boy climbed down and headed for Donna Cory's wagon. Effinger's wagon moved into position for the next ferry crossing and stopped. MacIvers grinned faintly to himself. If the troopers didn't find anything in Peebles' wagon, their suspicions would be dulled by two such staunch Northern families as the Wilcoxes and the Effingers.

He approached his own wagon. Abel held the reins and Coulter sat beside him. Abel seemed calm, but Coulter's eyes were fixed nervously on the search, still in progress on the other side. He looked at MacIvers and said, "If they find anything——"

MacIvers interrupted, "They won't. If they do, you'll have time to get a horse and run."

Coulter flushed. "I wasn't——"

Abel spoke without turning his head. "Shut up."

MacIvers studied Abel's face briefly. Coulter was a blusterer, and treacherous, but he was mush inside. Abel was

30

different. Abel was tough and dangerous. MacIvers felt a sudden certainty that neither Coulter nor Abel were going along on this journey because they wanted to enlist in the Army of the Confederacy. They were here because they wanted the gold. When the time was right, they'd make their play for it.

He glanced across the river and saw Wilcox' wagon leaving the ferry. The troopers abandoned the search of Peebles' wagon, and he began to reload his belongings. MacIvers released a sigh of relief.

The worst was over. Now if Wilcox kept still about the wagon's weight. . . .

Lucy Effinger's face was peering out again from the rear of her father's wagon, watching John Busby on the seat of Donna Cory's wagon. The ferry returned slowly and Effinger's wagon drove onto it.

MacIvers wondered at his own continuing uneasiness. Everything seemed to be going well enough. Yet he felt as though the wagons were carrying explosives that might go off at any time. Indeed, there was plenty of explosiveness in a train carrying people of such violently differing political beliefs. When enough time had passed, when the boredom of the journey began to be felt, there would surely be quarreling. And if anyone ever discovered what the wagons were carrying. . . .

He shrugged and returned to the river bank. He watched Effinger drive off the ferry on the other side and saw the troopers surround it.

Effinger climbed down, spoke briefly to the lieutenant, crossed to Wilcox, and began talking to him, gesturing as he did. Chances were that before they reached Sacramento, Effinger would have the wagon train split squarely down the middle, Northern sympathizers on the one side, Southerners on the other. For a brief moment MacIvers almost wished they were in Indian country already. A threat from outside the train might serve to maintain the unity of those within it.

The morning wore on slowly. Wagon after wagon crossed. The troopers took longer than usual with the search of MacIvers' wagon, but eventually left it and moved on to the next.

As John Busby drove Donna Cory's wagon onto the ferry, MacIvers called, "Tell Abel to come back and help me with the mules. You come with him. It'll probably take three of us."

The boy nodded; the ferry pulled away. Abel came back on the next trip, riding a saddle horse. Young Busby, carrying a bridle, came with him.

31

MacIvers roped out a mule, and Busby bridled him. MacIvers said, "Get on him and lead the others out into the river. Abel and I will drive."

The boy mounted the mule bareback. MacIvers dropped the rope corral and coiled up the rope while Abel eased the loose mules toward the river. He remounted and rode after them.

The mules balked at the bank, but John Busby forced his mule into the water. The others followed reluctantly, urged on from behind by the loud yells of MacIvers and Abel. They reached the far bank at the same time the ferry did.

It was almost noon. Locke's wagon, the last, climbed the bank from the ferry, and MacIvers rode down and paid the ferryman. The cavalry lieutenant's search of Locke's wagon was perfunctory. He gave MacIvers a casual salute, called, "Good luck, folks," and rode away.

MacIvers stared after them. Then, standing in his stirrups, he waved the wagons north.

Following the Sacramento, they crawled northward through choking clouds of dust. The sun climbed steadily. Driven by young Busby, the mules followed docilely.

Donna Cory, MacIvers noticed as he rode past, was pale. He dismounted, tied his horse behind her wagon, and motioned for her to halt her teams. He climbed up beside her. "I'll drive for you."

She smiled wanly. "Thank you. I'll be glad when we get into the mountains. It will be cooler there. After San Francisco, I'm not used to this heat."

There was silence between them for a while. At last she asked, "What were the soldiers looking for?"

"The lieutenant said contraband. But the ferryman said gold bullion. There have been a lot of robberies and raids, and none of the stolen gold has been found. They're searching every wagon train."

She was silent for a long time. At last she said, "It seems strange."

"What?"

"Riding here with you. My husband would have called you one of the enemy, because you come from Texas. What is it like down there?"

He grinned faintly. "We don't have slaves, if that's what you mean. The part of Texas I come from—it's brushy and dry and hot most of the time. We raise cattle and sometimes horses."

"What was she like—your wife, I mean?"

He frowned faintly, and she said immediately, "I'm sorry. It must hurt you to talk about her."

32

He shook his head. "You remind me of her sometimes."

"And she was raised in the North?"

"Pennsylvania," he lied.

"That's where we came from. What——"

He interrupted, "Your husband must have felt strongly to have left you and traveled across the country to enlist."

"He did. He——"

The wagon wheel on MacIvers' side dropped into a washout in the road and the wagon lurched. She was thrown against him, then thrown back as the wheel climbed out of the hole. He reached out a hand to steady her.

Her face was turned toward him and her eyes met his. And suddenly the hunger he had supressed all these months became overpowering. It was in his eyes, plain and undisguised.

Her face turned pale, then flushed. She tore her glance from his. She fixed her eyes on the endgate of the wagon just ahead.

The silence between them was awkward and painful. At last she said, "I feel better now. I'll be able to drive all right."

He nodded and handed her the reins. She halted the wagon, and he jumped down. He glanced up at her from the ground, but she wasn't looking at him.

Feeling vaguely angry, he untied his horse and mounted. As she drove away, he watched, stared hungrily at the curve of her throat, at her straight back, at her strong, small hands holding the reins. And though he cursed himself for his thoughts, he could not help wondering what it would be like to hold her in the night.

Busby's wagon passed him, enveloping him in a cloud of dust. He glanced up.

Busby was grinning knowingly at him. "Likely lookin' filly, ain't she, MacIvers? I wouldn't mind——" He stopped and glanced uneasily over his shoulder.

MacIvers turned his horse furiously and galloped toward the rear of the train. He told himself he was a fool. Yet his thoughts remained with Donna Cory the rest of that afternoon.

33

chapter 6

The journey up the Sacramento River was uneventful, but unbearably hot. They made good time. On the third day after leaving the San Joaquin, the lead wagon turned east toward the distant Sierras.

Effinger maintained an almost sullen silence about his stand on slavery, but he was friendly only with Wilcox. His manner toward Busby and Peebles was one of suspicious dislike.

Lucy Effinger carried water from the river every night, and most nights MacIvers would see John Busby heading for water at the same time she did. He grinned inwardly, wondering what her father would have to say about it if he knew.

The land rose steadily from Sacramento, and the going was slow. At noon each day, MacIvers had everyone change teams.

Behind the train trailed the extra mules, grazing at the side of the road, herded along by Coulter, who could ride even if he could not drive. John Busby and his father alternated at helping Donna Cory and Sally Bullock drive.

Climbing steadily through brushy hills, they covered no more than fifteen miles a day. The hills were littered with stumps and with the branches of giant redwoods cut by the settlers in Sacramento for lumber.

And then, one morning, they were in virgin timber. Shortly thereafter, they struck the canyon of Bear River, which they would follow to the crest of the Sierra Nevada.

Traveling slowed down as the grade increased, and the weight of the wagons became more noticeable. Once, Wilcox said as MacIvers was riding past, "This is the heaviest damn wagon I ever drove, or else these are the weakest mules."

34

MacIvers said, "Maybe you've got too much stuff, Mr. Wilcox."

"No more'n I had comin' west. Less, in fact. I can't figger it out."

MacIvers dropped back behind his own wagon, which Abel was driving. He frowned slightly as he watched the man.

Abel sat straight on the wagon seat, his expression as wooden as usual. Yet there seemed to be an alertness about him not apparent before today. Instead of staring straight ahead as he usually did, his eyes kept shifting from the road ahead to the nearby peaks whenever they were visible through the screening trees.

MacIvers told himself, "Things have been going too smooth. I'm looking for trouble where there isn't any." But his uneasiness did not subside, and he kept an eye on Abel whenever he could.

Coulter's arm apparently bothered him little now, except for the discomfort of having it in a sling. And his manner changed. From an attitude of surly resentment, it became one of arrogance that was almost triumphant.

They were planning something, MacIvers thought as he halted the wagons for the night.

The spot was one in which the narrowness of the canyon did not permit the wagons to form a circle as they usually did. Instead, they were strung out along the side of the cascading stream. On both sides the hills rose, rocky and precipitous.

While the travelers unhitched their teams, MacIvers rode ahead to scout the next day's route. He found himself studying the ground as he rode.

What, exactly, did he suspect, he wondered. That Coulter and Abel were expecting someone, he decided. That there would be an attack on the wagon train by friends of the pair.

Yet the idea of an impending attack seemed incomprehensible. The sheer physical weight of the gold ruled it out. How would the attackers escape with it? How would they transport eight tons of gold? Perhaps they wouldn't. Perhaps they'd cache it somewhere nearby. But even that was impractical. You couldn't carry eight tons of gold to a hiding place without leaving an obvious trail doing so.

He returned to camp. Fires were going now. He noticed that Sally Bullock was staring unwinkingly at Locke, a dozen yards away.

MacIvers stopped beside her, looking down. "You seem to know him. Do you?"

"I know him." She looked up, her expression changing instantly.

He waited, unspeaking, and at last she said, "I came west with him. He tells a beautiful story, Mr. MacIvers. About all the wealthy miners waiting in California for wives. He makes it sound so wonderful and adventurous. But when you get there, there aren't any rich miners waiting for you. There are only the saloons, and worse." Her voice was bitter and angry now.

He didn't know what to say. He touched the brim of his hat and moved on.

Coulter and Abel had a fire going. Coffee was boiling in a pot, and Abel was turning some deer-meat steaks. MacIvers squatted and stared at the leaping flames. He could hear the mules biting and kicking within their rope enclosure.

Mules, he thought. If you had enough mules with pack-saddles, you wouldn't have to follow roads and well-traveled trails. You could cut across country and head straight for Mexico.

Eighty to a hundred mules could carry all the gold. And now he realized something else. Perhaps they were willing to settle for less than all of it. They might take half, or even less, depending on how many of them there were.

He slept very little that night, waking at each small noise. He arose at dawn, a little surprised that nothing had happened during the night.

Perhaps, he thought, he was using his imagination too much. But he did not really believe it. It would happen some other night.

All day they toiled up the precipitous, narrow canyon, sometimes moving rocks in order to get through. MacIvers added an extra team of mules to each wagon at noon, for the road seemed to pitch upward even more sharply than before.

In midafternoon they reached a spot where the river, now only a creek, dropped in a waterfall for nearly a hundred feet. The road left the canyon bottom and in two sharp switch-backs ascended to the top of the falls.

Here, because of the danger of falling rocks, MacIvers sent the wagons up one at a time.

Busby's wagon happened to be traveling first. With the eight mules straining and lunging against the harness, it nego-tiated the first sharp turn and started up the first switchback.

MacIvers watched. Wheels perilously close to the edge, the huge wagon lumbered along, sometimes nearly slowing to a stop, sometimes lurching wildly on the rocky road.

Small rocks, dislodged by the straining mules, rolled down the slope, bounded across the road, and splashed into the stream. The wagon reached the second switchback.

Here Busby stopped, locking his brake, allowing the mules

to blow. John leaped down and chocked the wheels with rocks.

Wilcox grumbled, "If we all make it, it will be a miracle. These wagons are too damned big."

Above, Busby released the brakes and whipped his mules into motion. Young Busby stayed on the ground, ready to chock the wheels again if it was necessary.

Once more the huge wagon lumbered on, too wide for the road, seeming sometimes to be about to tip into the chasm below. Eventually, however, it reached the top and disappeared from sight.

Locke's wagon was next. The man's jaws were clenched as he started up.

MacIvers rode along behind, and each time Locke would stop, he dismounted hurriedly and chocked the wheels.

Sometimes the uphill wheels of the wagon were forced to climb the slope to avoid letting the downhill wheels roll off the road. Each time they did, the wagon tipped perilously.

For the first time, MacIvers was grateful for the weight of the gold in the wagon bed. The wagons were less top-heavy with it there.

It seemed to take an hour for the wagon to reach the top. Locke pulled it up behind Busby's wagon, locked the brake, and released a long sigh. He was sweating heavily and his eyes were scared. "Couple of times there I didn't think I'd make it at all. I was ready to jump."

MacIvers said, "Busby, you come on back. You can bring Mrs. Cory's wagon up." He started down the road, Busby following him on foot.

He had not yet reached the first switchback when he suddenly heard the crack of a rifle from above. It echoed back and forth between the canyon walls until it sounded like a dozen shots.

He whirled his horse and sank his spurs into the animal's sides. The horse nearly lost his footing as he plunged upward on the rocky ground, but recovered and went on. Busby stared after him confusedly.

Again a rifle sounded from above. Even before MacIvers heard the report, he saw the puff of smoke and heard the bullet strike the rocks beside him and whine off into space.

Leaning low, he yanked out his revolver, although he was not yet in range. He had not expected to be attacked in broad daylight. But what better place than this? What better place to hold the others back while they made off with over a million in gold, carried by the two wagons which had already reached the top?

Again and again the rifle roared. One of the bullets shattered

37

close to MacIvers' head and he felt the fragments sting his cheek. He felt the warmth of blood trickling down his face.

He reached the top and left his horse instantly, rolling through the cruelly cutting rocks for the shelter of some larger ones. A bullet threw a shower of rock fragments into his face, momentarily blinding him. He howled, "Locke! John! You all right?"

He got no reply and rubbed his eyes furiously until he could see again. Then he leaped to his feet and charged toward the pile of rock that had sheltered the rifleman.

The rifle roared, almost in his face. But he saw the man clearly, saw the low-pulled hat and the bandanna mask.

He fired instantly. The outlaw was driven back by the sheer force and weight of the heavy .44-caliber slug. MacIvers whirled around.

Locke was sitting on his wagon seat, hands raised in the air. John Busby was nowhere to be seen. Midway between the two wagons, three horsemen sat their mounts, guns in hands. And beyond the three horsemen were a dozen or more pack mules.

Zigzagging as he ran, MacIvers put Locke's wagon between the three and himself. He heard someone yell, "The son of a bitch got Ross!"

He rolled beneath Locke's wagon. From a prone position he poked his revolver out and fired point-blank at the nearest of the three.

The man dropped his revolver; it discharged as it struck the ground. Suddenly, behind them, a rifle poked through the canvas opening of Busby's wagon and roared deafeningly.

The horse of the one in the middle pitched forward, front legs folding. The man sitting him slid off and jumped clear. The horse rolled onto his side and lay there kicking, while blood ran from a gaping wound in his neck.

Still holding his gun, the man whirled and put two shots into the canvas of Busby's wagon. He turned and pointed the gun at Locke.

Locke yelled frantically, "No! That wasn't me! Don't."

MacIvers fired again. The man on the ground whirled from the force of the slug striking him in the shoulder. One of the mounted men bawled, "To hell with it! Come on!"

The two horses whirled and scrambled over the rocks toward the waiting mules. The man on the ground ran after them.

MacIvers could have killed him, but he held his fire. The wounded man snatched the trailing reins of the dead man's horse and scrambled to the saddle, awkward because of his wound. The three horses thundered away up the road.

MacIvers crawled from beneath the wagon. Young Busby's frightened face appeared at the rear of his father's wagon. MacIvers asked, "You hurt?"

The boy shook his head. MacIvers glanced at Locke. "How about you?"

Locke tried to speak, but all he could make were a few incoherent sounds.

MacIvers walked back to where the outlaw lay. Reaching down, he pulled the bandanna off the dead man's face. It was Rossiter, who had been with Brody, Coulter, and Abel the night MacIvers arrived at Brody's house in San Francisco.

Holstering his gun, he bent and grasped Rossiter beneath the shoulders. He dragged him about twenty feet to the concealment of some rocks. Turning, he said, "No use getting everybody all stirred up."

So far, neither young Busby nor Locke had asked what the outlaws wanted. Apparently neither had wondered what was valuable enough in the two wagons to prompt the robbery. But the question would come up. That was a certainty.

The pack mules left by the outlaws were restless, frightened by the shots and the smell of blood.

MacIvers said, "Be sure your brakes are set. Then come give me a hand. We can use these mules."

The pair climbed down. Locke's face still had not regained its normal color. Young Busby walked unsteadily. He grinned shakily at MacIvers. "I sure was scared."

MacIvers grinned back. "Can't blame you for that. You did the right thing at the right time, and that's all that counts."

The mules were tied in a string, halter rope of one tied to the tail of the one ahead. MacIvers picked up the halter rope of the lead mule and led the string into a grove of scrub trees at the stream bank. Assisted by Locke and John Busby, he removed the packsaddles and dumped them in a pile on the ground, saying, "We can't use these, and there's not much use taking them along."

Busby asked, his voice still not normal, "What were they after? We ain't got any money with us."

MacIvers answered without looking up. "They must have been freighters, judging from this string of pack mules. Maybe they were broke. Maybe they decided to hold us up on the spur of the moment, just to get a little cash."

Young Busby seemed to accept the explanation. But MacIvers doubted if the other members of the train would accept it unquestioningly.

He finished unsaddling the mules, took the halter rope of the lead animal, and led him up the road far enough so that the others were strung out in a line behind. He tied the mule to a tree. Returning, he said, "John, go back and help your father bring the next wagon up. I think maybe I'd best stay here."

Busby nodded and walked on down the road. MacIvers reloaded his gun. He doubted if Rossiter's friends would try again, but he didn't intend to make it easy for them if they did.

chapter 7

One by one the huge wagons lumbered up the steep-pitched road, negotiated the switchbacks, and arrived safely at the top. Peebles' wagon was third. Immediately following it came Wilcox', and after it Effinger's. As soon as he had locked his ratchet brake, Effinger called, "MacIvers!"

MacIvers rode to the side of the wagon. He looked up questioningly.

Effinger's face was cold. "There's something going on that we ought to know about. Why would these bandits risk their lives to rob two wagons in this train? What are those two wagons carrying?"

MacIvers shrugged. "Ask Busby and Locke. The wagons were searched back at the San Joaquin River. So far as I know they're not carrying anything valuable."

"I don't believe that, Mr. MacIvers. And there's another thing. These wagons are too big and expensive for what they're carrying. I believe we're all just being used."

MacIvers made his expression patient and questioning. "In what way, Effinger? You're going to get where you want to go. Is that being used?"

Effinger scowled. "I don't trust you, MacIvers. I——"

"Why don't you trust me? Because I'm from Texas? Because you suspect me of Southern sympathies? I've told you before and I'll tell you again. Keep the war out of this wagon train. Keep your politics to yourself."

"I think maybe it's time we elected another wagon master. One who will find out what's wrong in this wagon train."

MacIvers shrugged wearily. The last wagon, that of Donna Cory, had just arrived at the top. Standing in his stirrups, he waved the lead wagon on.

He started away, and Effinger yelled after him, "You're

41

going to abandon us out in the wilderness. You're picking up another cargo someplace, aren't you, MacIvers?"

MacIvers didn't reply. One by one the wagons rumbled on. Effinger started his, still glaring at MacIvers suspiciously. Behind the last wagon came the mules, with Coulter driving them.

MacIvers waited for him. He said, "Your friend Rossiter is dead."

"What the hell are you talking about?"

"He was one of the bunch that held us up."

"The hell he was! I'll bet him an' Carmichael—I knew I shoulda got rid of 'em both." He glanced at MacIvers' face and grinned. "One of them bullets came pretty close, didn't it? Too bad it wasn't closer."

MacIvers rubbed at the blood on his face with a sleeve. He stared at Coulter a moment more, then shrugged. "Pick up that string of mules that's tied to a tree up ahead. Drive 'em along with these. We can use some extras."

He whirled his horse and rode forward alongside the lumbering wagons. Coulter had put on a pretty convincing show of innocence. Yet he was sure that both Coulter and Abel had known. And if they had, they'd try again.

Furthermore, he would have to expect increasing opposition from Effinger. And if these overloaded wagons had barely been able to negotiate the switchbacks just below, what would they do when the going really got rough?

His persistent feeling of impending disaster angered him. He clenched his jaws. The wagons were going through if he had to pull them through himself.

Twice more that afternoon he had to send the wagons one at a time over a particularly steep stretch of road. By nightfall they had covered less than eight miles.

He found a spot to camp where the stream wandered through a mountain meadow, and he had the wagons form a tight circle. He sent Abel out to hunt for meat, but no sooner had Abel left than he saddled a fresh horse for himself and followed. If the outlaws were still around, Abel would find them. And if he did, MacIvers wanted to know.

The trail followed the wagon road for several miles, then left it and cut across one of the towering peaks. He followed another couple of miles before he heard a shot. He went on, crested a rise, and was able to see Abel a mile or so beyond, kneeling beside the carcass of a deer.

MacIvers turned his horse and rode back toward camp, relieved that for the time being, at least, he need not worry about outside threats.

Inside the circle of wagons the travelers were grouped.

No fires had been built and no preparations made for supper. Effinger was standing on his wagon, towering above the others like a bearded patriarch. He yelled as MacIvers rode into the circle, "Here he is! Ask *him* what's going on."

MacIvers stared up at him disgustedly. "Damn you, Effinger. I told you to keep your big mouth shut."

Effinger leaped to the ground. He shrugged out of his coat. "Suppose you shut it then." He turned his head and looked compellingly at the crowd. "This is as good a way as any to settle this!" he shouted. "If he wins, he's still the wagon boss. If he doesn't, I am. Agreed?"

The men in the crowd nodded approval. MacIvers glanced at them individually. Wilcox seemed confused, like a man who has been talked into something against his will. Locke was grinning, looking forward to the fight. Peebles and Busby were frowning, wondering if they shouldn't have taken a stronger stand.

Without his coat, Effinger looked bigger than he had with it on. He might be violent in his views, but it looked like he had the brawn to back them up.

MacIvers caught a glimpse of Coulter's face. The man was grinning slightly; it was plain who he wanted to see beaten into the ground. Coulter's purpose, which MacIvers was convinced was to steal part of the gold for himself, would be well served by disunion within the train.

Effinger took a classic boxer's stance. MacIvers approached cautiously.

While he was still ten feet away, Effinger let out a wordless shout and rushed. His left jabbed, and his right came whistling around with almost unbelievable speed, hitting the top of MacIvers' head.

Immediately Effinger dropped his hands and threw his body against MacIvers', bowling him back, to fall sprawling almost at Coulter's feet.

MacIvers rolled. He wasn't hurt, and he had learned what he needed to know about his adversary. Effinger was a boxer, but he was a brawler too. He was a lumber-camp fighter who knew all the tricks and who wouldn't quit until either he or MacIvers was unconscious.

Effinger rushed, swinging a heavy boot. Rising, MacIvers caught it and held it long enough to dump Effinger on the ground half a dozen feet beyond. He was up then, and rushing himself, he landed on Effinger's midsection with both knees.

Effinger's breath expelled violently. His hands clawed at MacIvers' face. MacIvers, no stranger to brawling himself, seized his beard with both hands and began methodically to beat his head against the ground.

43

Effinger doubled, then straightened himself like a whip. MacIvers was flung back. He rolled again, getting hands and knees under him, and came swiftly to his feet. Effinger, only a bit slower, made it up before MacIvers could rush. Warily now, they circled each other, looking for an opening.

Effinger's eyes gleamed with an almost fanatical fury. His mouth was a thin, straight line. Weary of circling, he rushed like a maddened buffalo.

His weight, striking MacIvers squarely, bore him helplessly back for a second time. He slammed into one of the rear wagon wheels and was momentarily held there by Effinger's momentum and weight. His gun, knocked out of its holster by the impact, fell to the ground at his feet.

Effinger's knee came up, and for an instant the pain was excruciating. MacIvers' head grew light and his vision blurred.

But with the pain came anger. The fight suddenly became a personal thing to him.

Pushing against the wagon wheel, he flung Effinger away and followed, chopping savagely at Effinger's unprotected face, hearing the solid, meaty sound as each blow struck.

Off balance, Effinger staggered back. Both MacIvers and Effinger were breathing hard, sweating heavily. Effinger recovered and once more assumed his boxer's stance. That whistling right swung for a second time, and this time it struck squarely.

Numbed by the force of it, MacIvers retreated. Coulter's outstretched foot tripped him, and his head struck a wagon spoke. He slumped against the wheel. And Effinger rushed, again swinging his heavy boot. It struck MacIvers' thigh, numbing his entire leg. But it also drove him, rolling, beneath the wagon, where he laid for an instant, shaking his head and trying to clear it.

Effinger dived beneath the wagon after him, clawing along the ground like an animal.

MacIvers rolled ahead of him, came out from beneath the wagon, and pulled himself up on the far rear wheel. As Effinger came out after him, he swung a boot. It caught Effinger on the shoulder, but it didn't stop the man. He stood up, holding a heavy wagon jack in both his hands. He was completely wild with rage. In this moment he was fighting slavery as well as MacIvers personally, and if he killed, he would be able to justify it to himself in the name of the cause.

Still dizzy, still unsteady, MacIvers knew he had to avoid that heavy jack if he did nothing else. It would split his skull like an egg, or break a bone wherever it happened to strike.

It was heavy, even for Effinger. Veins standing out on his streaming forehead from effort and exertion, Effinger swung the jack. It started ponderously, coming up in an arc. As it swung, it gained speed. If he could avoid it, its weight would swing Effinger completely around.

MacIvers ducked low, too late for Effinger to change the direction of his swing. He felt the thing go past his head, felt the rush of air it made. He straightened.

The heavy jack's momentum swung Effinger around. And as it did, MacIvers plunged forward, swinging his right fist with all the force of his forward moving body, with all the waning strength left in him.

It struck the back of Effinger's neck. Already off balance from the weight of the swinging jack, Effinger staggered away and fell in a heap on top of the jack. He laid there completely still.

Head hanging, lungs working like a bellows, MacIvers stumbled to the wagon wheel and clung there helplessly. His head whirled. He scarcely heard the babble of voices filling the clearing on the other side of the wagon to which he clung.

Effinger stirred and groaned. His wife went to him, turned him over, and began to bathe his face with water. Donna Cory came to MacIvers and asked softly, her voice shocked, "Are you all right? Is there anything——"

He shook his head wearily. He had stopped Effinger's attempt to take over as wagon boss. That was all that mattered to him. But even in this exhausted moment of triumph he knew how temporary his victory had been. Effinger's convictions wouldn't change. Nor would his suspicions be quieted. If ever one of the wagons was wrecked, if ever the bullion was found. . . .

He pushed himself away from the wagon wheel and forced himself to stand erect. He swayed slightly, but refused Donna Cory's steadying hand.

He walked between the wagons and faced the group. "Build your fires and eat," he said. "The trail will probably be worse tomorrow."

They scattered silently. He turned and headed for the stream. Donna Cory blocked his way. "I'd be pleased if you'd have supper with me tonight, Mr. MacIvers."

"Those," he said, "are the pleasantest words I've heard tonight." He walked carefully toward the stream to duck his head in its icy water and to wash the grime and blood from his hands and face.

chapter 8

Donna Cory was preparing supper over a fire beside her wagon. She looked up as MacIvers approached. Her expression was a strange mixture of confusion, puzzlement, and disapproval. Yet there was something else in her eyes.

He said, "You don't think I should have fought with Effinger."

Her face flushed faintly, and she returned her glance to the fire. But she shook her head.

He said, "If I hadn't, Effinger would have become wagon master. Do you think he would have done a better job?"

She looked up again. "That wasn't what I thought. Maybe it seems to me there ought to be a better way to deciding things. Like who is to boss this wagon train. And like whether the South should be made up of slave states or free. My husband—he had never seen a slave, Mr. MacIvers. Yet he's dead because of them."

He leaned against a wagon wheel. "There's more to it than slavery, I think. To the South, ma'am, it's a matter of—" He hesitated. "I dislike comparing human beings to animals, but suppose Washington were to say suddenly that it was unlawful for a citizen to own a mule. Or a horse. And that all of them henceforth were free."

Her expression, while mirroring his disapproval of the comparison, nevertheless showed that she saw his point. She nodded reluctantly. "I think I see what you mean. That the slaveholders became slaveholders legally. And that by suddenly making slavery unlawful, they are deprived of their property without due process."

"That's pretty close." He grinned suddenly. "Now you'll say I sound like a rebel."

"Aren't you, Mr. MacIvers?"

His grin widened. "Maybe I am. It would be a pretty poor man who didn't stand and be counted with his neighbors and his friends."

"But you're not fighting with them."

"You're not being consistent now. You just said there ought to be a better way of settling things."

She smiled, and suddenly all the disapproval was gone from her eyes. "It's time to eat."

He pushed himself away from the wagon wheel. She turned her head and looked up at him.

Again she reminded him of his wife. The way she turned her head, the half smile lingering on her lips. His face sobered and for an instant their glances locked.

He accepted the plate from her and squatted on his heels. He ate silently. Abel rode into the circle of wagons, the deer hung across his horse's rump. He dismounted, dumped the carcass on the ground, and led his horse away toward the rope corral.

MacIvers called, "Wilcox! Busby! Skin it out and hang it in a tree."

He turned his head and found Donna Cory watching him. She said suddenly, "I think perhaps you ought to know the things people are saying."

He said, "I have some idea, I think, but I'd like to know."

She hesitated, obviously feeling vaguely disloyal for speaking so. Then she said firmly, "They are saying that something is wrong with this wagon train. The wagons are too big for what they are carrying and for the mountain trails. There are more wagons than we need. Mr. Effinger believes you are going to abandon us out in the wilderness and pick up another load."

"Another load of what?"

She smiled faintly. "He doesn't know. He believes it is something to do with the war, although what eight wagons could carry that would materially affect the course of the war, I can't imagine."

She was getting too close, thought MacIvers. He said quickly, "I think somebody might have done a better job of choosing the people for this train. They should either have been all Northern sympathizers or all Southern. It's the mixture that's causing trouble."

"Perhaps you're right." He was relieved that he had diverted her thoughts from what the wagons might be carrying or what they might be meant to carry later on. If her thoughts on that and Wilcox' certainty that the wagons were overly heavy came together. . . .

Slowly the camp quieted as one after another of the travelers sought their beds. The fire died to a bed of coals.

MacIvers was reluctant to leave. He felt relaxed, at peace with himself in her company. But at last he rose. "We're near the top of the range. Tomorrow won't be any easier."

"I suppose not." He felt a reluctance in her that matched his own.

They faced each other for a moment, only inches apart. Suddenly MacIvers bent his head and touched her lips lightly with his own. "Good night."

He turned and walked away, hearing faintly her soft reply, "Good night."

He got his blankets out of the wagon and rolled himself in them. He stared at the stars above.

Nearby, Abel grunted, "I hear I missed a good scrap."

MacIvers didn't reply.

From beyond Abel, Coulter said, "You might have missed the scrap, but it don't look like MacIvers is missing anything."

MacIvers grunted, "Shut up."

Coulter muttered something under his breath, turned in his blankets, and softly cursed the discomfort caused by his splinted arm.

So far, MacIvers thought, the two single women in the train had caused no serious trouble. But they had only started the journey east.

But he'd meet that problem when it arose. Now there were other things.

He slept at last, alert as always and hearing each small noise.

From here, the road pitched upward ever more steeply. The trail grew narrower and more rocky than before. Today there were many grades where each wagon required six teams of mules.

It was made clear to MacIvers that while he had beaten Effinger the night before, he had lost what little support he had previously enjoyed from the two families of Northern sympathizers within the group. Wilcox and his wife stared at him coldly. Effinger was sullen, looking at him with angry, smoldering eyes.

The lines were drawn, he thought, and henceforth there would be two clearly marked sides within the wagon train. Yet even that, he realized, was not without its advantages. At least the two groups would keep to themselves whenever possible.

He drove for Donna Cory. And he detailed John Busby to drive for Sally, grinning at the way John's face flushed as he climbed to the seat beside her.

At noon, he sighted another wagon train high on the narrow shelf road above. He halted the wagons at a spot where they could pull aside, and they waited expectantly for the other train to pass.

It was a large train, composed of twenty-three wagons. An hour after they had pulled aside, the first wagon drew abreast.

The driver halted it, and the occupants climbed out and mingled with the members of MacIvers' train, who asked eagerly for news of the war.

MacIvers rode between the two trains, anxious to get started again, but unwilling to break up the gathering too soon.

Young Busby, he noticed, had stayed on Sally's wagon seat. He rode on ahead and saw Sally coming toward her wagon, holding up her skirt so that she wouldn't trip. She glanced at him, flushed, and looked away. She passed him without looking up at him again.

MacIvers turned his head and watched her climb to the seat of her wagon, assisted by a red-faced John Busby. He frowned. On impulse he rode on forward until he reached Locke's wagon, the fourth beyond Sally's.

He stared at the wagon thoughtfully. Then he shook his head. Sally had made clear how she felt about Jack Locke. Yet what could she do in a few minutes' time?

The wagon master of the other train bawled an order to proceed and the two groups separated reluctantly. The other train moved past and MacIvers' wagons took to the road again. Jolting upward, they climbed the steep and narrow trail.

In midafternoon, they reached another series of switchbacks like those they had climbed just before the attack the day before. Again MacIvers sent the wagons up one by one.

Today it was Donna Cory's wagon that went up first. Tying his horse behind, MacIvers climbed to the seat and took the reins.

The teams lunged ahead, digging in, scrambling, scattering rocks behind their shod hoofs. The wagon jolted ahead, seemingly only inches at a time. He halted often, setting the brake, giving the mules a chance to rest.

He reached the top at last, pulled ahead enough to give the other wagons room to stop at the top, set the brake, and climbed down. He untied his saddle horse, mounted, and started down the road.

Busby was already to the first switchback. He drove with a confidence he had not displayed the day before.

MacIvers waited until he reached the top. Then he started

down, suddenly remembering Locke's white-faced fear of the switchback trail they had negotiated yesterday.

Locke's teams started up. MacIvers could hear the rattle of small rocks kicked loose by the mules. Locke reached the first switchback. Suddenly he stood up and fought frantically with the brake. MacIvers dug spurs into his horse's sides. Sally! Damn her, she'd done something to Locke's brake.

His horse plunged ahead. Once he went to his knees on the rocky road, nearly throwing MacIvers clear. MacIvers yanked him around a switchback, forced now to turn his head in order to see Locke.

A brake tampered with, a wrecked wagon, splintered fifty feet below, and every member of the train would know what was wrong with this wagon train. The gold bars would lie scattered with the wreckage.

Locke had dropped his reins to fight the brake. The mules, without control, were trying desperately to hold the wagon's weight. Two of them were plunging, fighting the harness, and perilously close to the edge.

MacIvers yelled, "Locke! Stay with it! Forget the brake and get hold of your reins!"

Locke's face, turned suddenly toward him, was gray. The man abandoned his attempts to set the brake. He leaped off the wagon on the uphill side, clawing like an animal up the precipitous slope.

Leaving the road, MacIvers sent his fighting, plunging horse directly across the hillside above the road. Rocks cascaded from the horse's scrambling feet. The animal uttered a snort of terror. He tried to balk, but MacIvers spurs forced him on.

A hundred yards—fifty yards—and Locke's straining mules still held the wagon's weight.

Twenty-five yards. The wagon began to roll back, its wheels turning toward the edge.

MacIvers kept forcing his horse ahead. He bawled a stream of profanity at the mules. It steadied them briefly. In that instant, MacIvers left his saddle, making a flying leap for the wagon seat below.

He straightened, fighting his way up, clawing for the reins. Some were lost, dragging on the ground between the teams. Under his breath he cursed Locke savagely. Turning his head, he yelled, "You dumb son of a bitch, get down off there and put a rock behind the wheel!"

He didn't wait to see if Locke would comply. He leaped to the back of the nearest mule. Clinging to one hame, he leaned low and scooped up the dangling reins.

A wheel went off the edge and the huge wagon tilted perilously. MacIvers shouted a stream of curses, got the reins straightened out, and saw the mules dig in and lunge ahead.

The wheel hung over the edge. Rocks cascaded from the hoofs of the straining mules. MacIvers yelled again.

Slowly the wagon rolled ahead; slowly it righted itself. It inched onward up the grade.

MacIvers yelled again at Locke and saw the man slide down to the road behind the wagon. A moment later he faintly heard a wordless shout from Locke.

He let up on the teams gradually, felt the wagon roll back slightly and stop. He released a long sigh of relief.

Now he turned his attention to the brake. A pin had been removed from it and was lying on the floor at MacIvers' feet.

He picked it up and slipped it into place. He set the brake. He'd key the pin when he reached the top.

He gave the mules a ten-minute rest, then drove on toward the top, still sweating heavily. His horse, having picked his way down to the road, followed along behind.

At the top, he keyed the brake pin, then mounted and rode, still furious, toward the bottom. He stopped beside Sally Bullock's wagon and glared at her. "If you have to kill him, do it with a gun. Don't kill half the people in the train trying to get at him."

Her face was white and scared, but her eyes were cold. "I will use a gun next time, Mr. MacIvers. I can promise you I will. And I'll kill him before we reach the Missouri. I can also promise that."

chapter 9

One by one the wagons fought their way up the steep grade to the top. They camped here, and for a couple of hours before dark, MacIvers, John Busby, and Abel loose-herded the mules in a mountain meadow half a mile off the road, allowing them to graze. The night passed without incident.

Day followed day as they toiled up the ever steepening road, which now could scarcely be called a road. Here, the weight and strength of the wagons paid off. Few stops were necessary for repairs.

The day came at last when the lead wagon ground to a halt at the summit of Donner Pass.

The wind was sharp, blowing out of the north. The air was clear. MacIvers sat his horse beside the lead wagon, staring at the dim horizon and at the road, no more than a narrow trail, dropping precipitously to be lost in the deep canyons thousands of feet below.

For a moment he wondered if they would make it through the primitive country ahead. He turned his head and stared at the wagons, toiling upward toward this spot. He frowned.

There was no unity among the people of the wagon train. Rarely did the members of the two opposing factions bother to speak civilly to each other. They had formed two separate camps and there was no intermingling.

MacIvers allowed them an hour at the top to rest. Then he waved them on. Damn them, he thought, if he kept them working hard enough, if he got them to the point of exhaustion and kept them there, they'd have no energy left for quarrels.

Down the other side they went, braking all the way, sometimes snubbing ropes to trees to ease the wagons down, sometimes chaining the great rear wheels so that they couldn't turn but could only slide.

The weight of the wagons became an extra liability now, and MacIvers realized on how thin a thread hung his chances of success. A broken snubbing rope, a single skid, a brake that failed—and one of these things could happen at any time. And if only one of them did happen, it would mean a wrecked wagon and disclosure to all within the train that the wagons were carrying contraband bullion.

If there was disunity now, it would become ten times worse. Gone would be any chance of concealing the purpose of the train from the Union troops they were certain to encounter along the way.

Both Abel and Coulter worked like madmen, obviously realizing the danger as well as MacIvers did. The two seemed to be everywhere, and whenever they were needed, they were there, manning a snubbing rope, jamming a rock ahead of a sliding wheel, standing hip-deep in the furiously rushing stream to calm or help the wildly plunging teams.

Twenty times a day the trail crossed the stream. Tempers grew short; flare-ups were frequent. MacIvers broke up at least three fights every day.

Sally Bullock grew thin and pale, but whenever Locke was within sight, her eyes rested on him with undiminished malevolence. And Locke grew ever more nervous. Three days from the summit he could stand it no longer and came to MacIvers as the wagons halted for the night.

"You got to do something about that damn woman. She said she was goin' to shoot me, and she will. Can't you search her stuff and get her guns away from her?"

"I don't even know that she's got a gun." MacIvers felt no sympathy for Locke but he knew he needed the man. Locke could drive. He was driving an eighth of the bullion. If anything happened to him. . . .

He shrugged. "All right. I'll take a look."

Reluctantly he walked to Sally Bullock's wagon. There were dark circles under Sally's eyes. He said bluntly, "I want your gun."

She stared at him without expression.

He said almost irritably, "I'm not taking his side, if that's what's bothering you. I just want him alive until we get to the Missouri. I need him. We've got few enough men as it is."

Still she didn't speak. He asked, "Are you sure he's worth it? There's a price on murder that you'll have to pay."

She spoke out suddenly, angrily, "Do you think I care? All I want is to see him pay the price."

"You told me what he was, but you didn't tell me he was a killer."

"Well, he is. And the law won't touch him for it."

53

He waited, not particularly anxious to hear her story, but aware that telling it would help her own state of mind.

She said, "I had a friend on the way out here. She didn't know what she was getting into any more than I did. When she found out, she was broke and she couldn't find anything to do except— Well, anyway she wouldn't do it. She jumped into the bay." Sally stopped, trembling. She met his eyes steadily. "Jack Locke killed her as surely as if he threw her into the bay himself. And I'm going to kill Jack Locke."

"That won't bring her back. And it won't undo what he did to you."

"But it will keep him from doing it to any others like us. You know why he's going east, don't you? To bring another wagon train of women out."

MacIvers said gently, "I have to get your gun if you have one. Do you want to give it up, or will I have to search?"

She stared at him a moment furiously. Then she shrugged. "All right. I'll give them up. But it won't stop me. It won't keep me from trying."

He waited. She climbed up to her wagon seat and rummaged beneath the canvas top. She handed down an ancient rifle and a pearl-handled derringer.

He felt almost ashamed for taking them. He turned, walked to his own wagon, and stowed them beneath some extra harnesses. Then he went toward the rushing, icy stream to wash.

He knelt, ducked his head in the water, and scrubbed vigorously. Standing, he dried his face on a flour sack he had brought along. He stood there, staring at the water, staring ahead at the descent they must attempt tomorrow.

He heard a murmur of voices and turned his head. Screened from him by brush and trees, he saw the dim forms of two people. They were embracing, and as he watched they broke away. He heard Lucy Effinger's voice faintly over the roar of the stream. "John, no! What if my father——"

"He'd just as well know now as later. He's got to know sometime."

"You don't know how he is. If you weren't——"

"From the South? I don't see what difference that makes. I love you, Lucy. I want to marry you."

"You don't know him. You just don't. No telling what he'd do."

"I'm not afraid of him."

"Well, I am. He might kill you. Or he might beat you." She stopped, and her voice took on a pleading note. "You saw how he was in the fight he had with Mr. MacIvers."

"We'll run away as soon as we get someplace where we can."

"He'd follow us, John. Can't we just go on seeing each other like we have been doing? Does he have to know? Can't we just be more careful?"

"I don't like it, hiding by the stream every night, acting like I don't even know you during the day."

MacIvers saw her stand on tiptoe and put her arms around John Busby's neck. He could not hear her words because they were softly spoken, but he could imagine what they were. He grinned faintly and headed for camp again. Then the grin faded, and a worried look came into his eyes. If Effinger did find out. . . .

He walked through the camp slowly and beyond to the small clearing where the mules were rope-corralled. Already the grass had been stripped from the ground within the enclosure.

He stared moodily at the listless animals. They had been worked too hard over the past two weeks, and fed too little. He wished that he'd brought a couple of tons of oats along. If they didn't get out of this high country soon, if they didn't reach flat country where there was grass for the mules. . . .

He returned to camp. The Effingers, the Wilcoxes and Donna Cory were on one side of it. The Busbys, the Peebles, Locke, Abel, and Coulter were on the other. Sally Bullock was cooking between the two groups.

A gloomy feeling came over him. The trail until now had been rough and steep and dangerous, but except for the outlaw attack upon Busby's and Locke's wagons, there had been no threat from outside the train.

That would change. They must travel through several hundred miles of hostile Indian country, and a train this small would tempt attack. He walked to Donna Cory's fire and stopped.

She glanced up unsmilingly. "Will you eat with me, Mr. MacIvers?"

He nodded and leaned against the rear wheel of her wagon, watching her. Her expression did not have its usual warmth as she said, "Mr. Effinger says he has it figured out. He says that you will turn the wagons south when we reach the Rocky Mountains. He believes you are going to abandon us somewhere and load the wagons with guns and ammunition which will have been gathered together by Southern sympathizers in Denver City. He then believes you will take the wagons on to Texas and turn the guns over to your friends, who will try another march up the Rio Grande as General Sibley did."

"Do you believe him?"

Her eyes were troubled. "I don't know what to believe. I think I could hate you if you deceived me. I think I would feel disloyal to my husband and to everything in which I believe if I helped make such a thing possible, even by my presence in this wagon train."

He said, "I was born in the South, Mrs. Cory. Would it be wrong for me to believe in their side of this conflict as deeply as you believe in the Northern cause?"

She frowned. "You're confusing me. I think it would be wrong for you to use me and the rest of these people to do whatever it is you plan to do. If, through you, more Union soldiers like my husband are to be killed and if you supply guns for the killing—"

"Effinger could be wrong."

She stared at him. "Is he wrong, Mr. MacIvers?"

He had no choice. He had to lie to her. And the fact that the lie was a technical one didn't help. He wasn't going to transport guns to Texas. But he was using her, and the others too.

He met her glance steadily. "Effinger is wrong, Donna. Neither you nor any of the others will be abandoned anywhere. The train is going to the Missouri. And it will carry no guns. Does that satisfy you?"

Her smile was like the sun coming out after a storm. She flushed, glanced down, and murmured, "Thank you. I'll tell Mr. Effinger that he is wrong."

"I wouldn't do that. He won't believe you anyway. Let him think what he thinks. At least it's keeping his mind occupied."

She looked up, smiling. "Perhaps you're right. Now come and eat."

He accepted a plate from her and squatted to eat. Across the fire he suddenly met Coulter's eyes. He caught the man off guard, surprising a hatred in Coulter's eyes that startled him. He had thought it might have cooled by now.

Coulter looked away and MacIvers studied Abel sitting beside him.

The man was an enigma. Silent almost to the point of sullen taciturnity, Abel's speech gave no clues to his character. Yet MacIvers felt sure he had known about the impending attack by Rossiter and his friends. He also felt sure Abel had meant to share in the loot. That ruled him out as a patriotic Southerner. And yet he didn't seem the greedy kind, as Coulter did, nor did he seem the type to care for either money or the things it bought.

He surprised Donna Cory studying him. Her face was as puzzled as his own must be, he thought.

She smiled helplessly, "I've been trying to understand you, and I can't. You look at your two friends as though you distrusted them. Why?"

He shrugged, and she went on. "They've been doing more work than anyone else in the train. It's almost as though they had a personal stake in it." He wished the conversation between them didn't always have to return to this.

She asked suddenly, "What will you do when you reach the Missouri?"

He shrugged. "Enlist, perhaps. Or bring another train of wagons west."

She stared soberly into the flames.

He asked, "And what will you do?"

She shook her head. "Go home, I suppose. Take up life as it was before I married. I don't really know what I want to do. I only—I suppose there were too many memories in California."

She got up and filled his coffee cup. He stood to drink it, watching as she cleared away the things she had used getting supper. She put them in a large pan, preparatory to taking them to the stream.

He touched the brim of his hat and put his coffee cup in the pan. "Thank you for the supper. Good night." He walked away toward his own wagon.

He had been unnecessarily abrupt and realized it. Yet he knew there could be no future in a relationship with her. When she knew that she and the others had been used to hide the true purpose of this trip, when she knew how important to the Southern cause it had really been. . . .

He turned and watched her walk into the darkness toward the rushing stream. And again he felt the hunger, the need that had troubled him ever since he had first met her.

He scowled and took his blankets from the wagon. He laid down and stared at the sky overhead.

The stream made a continuous roar. And the air grew chill.

Day followed day with backbreaking monotony as the wagons inched down the eastern slope of the Sierra range. The Truckee River grew in size as tributaries entered it, as it was fed by springs along the way. Crossing it became more difficult. Twice, men helping the plunging teams of weakened mules across were swept away, battered on the rocks, and nearly drowned.

They reached the foot of the mighty range and traveled

for several days in gradually flattening foothills. And now, for the first time in many days, the mules were able to graze.

At the point where the trail left the Truckee, MacIvers had all the water kegs washed out, filled, and checked for leaks. Then they started across open country, where most times they could see for thirty miles and where the going was relatively easy after the mountain trail.

But there was dust. And heat. And there was the never-ending hostility between the two opposing groups.

MacIvers thought of the thousand and more miles still lying ahead of them. He thought of the Rockies, still to be crossed, of the hostile Cheyenne and Arapaho. He thought of the desert between here and Salt Lake. He stared at the gaunt mules and knew they would not replace the weight they had lost on the mountain trails. Not in this heat. Not in the waterless desert ahead. He was glad they had as many extra mules as they did, but he couldn't help wondering if they had enough.

chapter 10

Endless monotony now became a traveler with the train. Their direction was northeast. MacIvers pushed them hard, trying each day for twenty miles, but rarely making it. Usually the distance covered by the day's end was fifteen miles or less.

Knowing the desert was ahead, he watched the mules and made sure they were herded where forage was the best. Sometimes he would have young Busby and Coulter, who usually herded them, halt them in a grassy spot where they could graze for a couple of hours before going on. Yet they gained none of the flesh they had lost in the Sierras. But for all that, they seemed strong enough.

Exhaustion cooled the tempers of the travelers, but it did not remove their differences. It only turned volatile anger into sullenness.

Sally Bullock was silent, driving her wagon with sleeves rolled to her elbows, her face intent and expressionless. Locke avoided her.

Effinger's face was like that of a brooding preacher who is surrounded by sin. His wife sat silently beside him on the wagon seat, or walked beside the wagon and watched the two smaller children playing along the way. The Wilcoxes watched the Effinger children, their eyes filled with longing and with pain.

Peebles whined about the heat, the dust, the miles that lay ahead. And Busby shirked whenever possible.

Abel remained an enigma. Donna Cory's face was pale with weariness.

Coulter took the splints off his arm, though MacIvers doubted if the bone had completely knit itself. He began to hang around the wagons of both Sally Bullock and Donna

Cory, helping them gather wood or buffalo chips when there was no wood, helping them build fires, putting himself out to be agreeable.

The miles fell behind. And the day came at last when MacIvers could see the thing he had dreaded all the way. The Salt Lake desert, eighty-two miles of flat, blistering salt, glaring in the sun, distorted by the heat waves rising from it.

They spent most of the day cutting grass and filling the wagons with loose hay. They filled the water kegs and every other vessel available. They drank their fill and allowed the mules to do the same.

MacIvers waited until sunset to start, knowing that only by traveling at night, resting by day, could he get both wagons and mules across. Yet even at night the heat was terrible. Sweat soaked the front and back of his shirt as he walked, leading his horse. His feet sank into the soft sand, which was mostly salt. So did the wide wagon wheels. At every stop, the mules would lick the ground for salt, which they had been long without. The drivers' efforts to force their heads up were in vain.

Salt would make the animals thirsty, MacIvers knew. He wished the mules had been provided with it all along the way.

Straining, lunging, the mules pulled the heavy wagons through the yielding sand. Sometimes a wagon would sink in half a foot. Stops to rest the mules became more frequent as the night progressed. When sunup came, MacIvers admitted to himself that they had covered less than ten miles.

Effinger came to him when they stopped. "We could have swung north and avoided this."

MacIvers stared at him. "There's no trail north of here. It'd take a month to get through it, and we haven't got a month. We might never get through."

"You've seen it then?"

MacIvers glanced at him irritably. "You know I haven't. But I've talked to men who have. It's rough country, cut up by canyons that all run north and south."

"What about south of here, then?"

"There's no more water south than there is right here. And the distance is greater."

Effinger stalked away, grumbling. He went to Wilcox' wagon and began to talk to him in undertones.

Most of the travelers ate a cold meal rather than build fires in the heat. Then they laid in their wagons' shade and tried to rest.

Few could sleep. MacIvers sat with his back against a wagon wheel, watching them. Nearby Abel laid on his back

60

and stared at the cloudless sky. Coulter watched Sally Bullock, lying not far away with a sunburned arm across her face. His face was intent, and occasionally he licked his lips.

Ten miles, MacIvers thought. Ten miles out of eighty-two. And as they continued, the distance covered each night would grow shorter. The mules would grow weaker. A few of them might die. If they got across in ten days, it would be a miracle.

He didn't know if their water would last ten days. He doubted if it would. If they ran out. . . .

He closed his eyes, but he did not sleep. His clothes were soaked with sweat. He listened unthinkingly for the sound of a water-keg cover being removed. Everyone had been told how the water was to be conserved. There was to be no washing. Drinking water was rationed, morning and night. Yet he knew there would be a few who would disregard the rules.

The day dragged endlessly. MacIvers slept in snatches, awaking at each small noise. At sundown Effinger and Wilcox came to him.

He looked up wearily. "What the hell is it now?"

Effinger scowled. "We think you ought to leave a couple of these wagons behind. You don't need them. The things they're carrying can be divided among the other six. It will save mules. It might save our lives."

MacIvers shook his head. "We'll keep 'em all."

"Why? Why are they so important?"

"Wagons cost money. That's one reason."

"Mules cost money too. If you lose ten mules, that's more than the cost of the wagons you'll save."

"No."

"Is there another reason, Mr. MacIvers? Won't six wagons be enough for the guns you're planning to take south to your rebel friends?"

MacIvers got up. He stared at Effinger disgustedly. "Why don't you shut up? If you're so damned anxious to boss a wagon train, then make one up when you reach Missouri. Bring it back this way. In the meantime keep your mouth shut about how this one is being run."

Effinger's face flushed furiously. His mouth became a thin line.

MacIvers shouted, "Hitch up! Let's get rolling!"

Almost sullenly the members of the group got up. They caught mules and hitched up, careful to use mules that had not been used the night before.

MacIvers helped Donna Cory, then Sally Bullock. Both women were listless. Sally smiled faintly as she said, "All I can seem to think about is that icy mountain stream. I hated it when we had to cross it a dozen times a day, but it would look mighty good right now."

He nodded, caught and saddled his horse, then led out, walking, leading the animal.

The sun was down, but its heat lingered in the sand. MacIvers' feet burned as he plodded along. The wagons followed, stringing out for a quarter mile.

He guided himself by the position of the North Star. Periodically he would pass the scattered bones of an ox, or a mule; or he would see a bed, or chair, faded but unbroken.

He could only guess at the miles they covered that night. Or the next.

As the days and nights passed, Peebles' complaining grew more insistent. Effinger's sullen bad temper became more potentially explosive. Even Wilcox, normally even-tempered, cursed sourly at the lagging mules.

The fourth evening, three of the mules could not get up. MacIvers shot them, and the train moved on.

Four halts were made that night to replace a mule that had collapsed in harness. By morning MacIvers estimated that half their water was gone. And he was short seven mules. He now had but one complete change of mules for the eight wagons. If he lost more, it would mean that some of the mules, the stronger ones, would have to pull a wagon two nights in a row.

And he did lose more. On the fifth night he lost seven. On the sixth night ten. The sixth night he guessed they covered no more than seven miles.

When dawn came, the wagons halted as usual. Effinger moved around through the camp, talking first to one, then another. Not long afterward he yelled, "All right! Let's go see about this right now!"

Effinger approached slowly, to be joined by the other members of the train. Wilcox. Busby and his son, John. Peebles. Donna Cory, Locke, and Sally Bullock. The wives of the married men walked in the rear of the group. Lucy Effinger stayed with her two younger brothers, who were both whimpering.

Behind MacIvers, Coulter reached into the wagon bed for a gun. He cocked it noisily. MacIvers wanted to tell him to put it away, but he did not. He reminded himself of the faltering Confederacy. He thought of how much good the bullion was going to do.

Effinger said, "We've had enough, mister. We're leaving two of these wagons behind. Mrs. Cory can ride with the Wilcoxes. Miss Bullock can ride with us."

MacIvers realized his own temper was wearing thin. He wanted to explode. Instead he forced his voice to be calm. "The answer is no. I'm sorry. All the wagons are going through. If we lose too many mules, a couple of us will ride on to the edge of this damn desert. We'll bring back more."

Wilcox spoke up. "Why? For God's sake, why? They're only wagons. You can get more in Salt Lake."

MacIvers said, "Call it stubbornness if you like. But all eight wagons are going through!"

"We can elect another wagon boss."

MacIvers nodded. "You can. But he won't take over because I won't let him."

Busby said, "Things can happen along the trail. You might not be around."

MacIvers pushed himself away from the wagon wheel. "Are you threatening me, Mr. Busby?"

"Not me. Don't get me wrong. I——"

"Then keep your mouth shut."

"You can't——"

"I can and I will. If there's any more of this sort of thing, I'll take your guns."

Effinger turned his head and looked at the others. "I told you there was something wrong with this wagon train. These wagons are either carrying something we don't know about, or they're going to carry something later on."

MacIvers said, "They were searched at the San Joaquin. You saw how carefully."

"Something's hollow then. There's something hidden in 'em someplace. I'd bet on it."

MacIvers felt cold. He hoped his face was as expressionless as his voice. He said, "Search 'em yourselves, then. If you'd rather do that than sleep. But when night comes, we're going on. Whether you've slept or not."

They looked at him with balked fury. Even Donna Cory's face was cold as her eyes met his. He turned his head. Coulter stood behind him, grinning, cocked rifle ready. Abel wasn't grinning, but he had a revolver in his hand.

MacIvers looked at Effinger. "They'll shoot if I give the word, Mr. Effinger."

Effinger's eyes burned. He knew that what MacIvers said was true. He took a backward step, grumbling.

The others broke, turned, and shuffled away separately. Abel said, "We'd better get their guns."

MacIvers shook his head. "Not yet."

The sun was rising, putting a blinding white glare on the desert. Heat waves began to rise, distorting the surface of the land. There was an ominous silence within the camp.

Abel grunted, "What if they do start looking? What if they find——"

MacIvers said, "What if they do? Will they be any harder to handle than they are right now? Besides that, I doubt if they'll find anything."

Effinger got a hammer out of his wagon. He crossed to Wilcox, who had another. The two began to tap on the wagon spokes, one by one, listening carefully for hollow sounds.

Coulter said worriedly, "You better stop 'em, MacIvers. They're getting too damned close."

"If I do, they'll be sure they're getting close."

"Maybe, but what if they look——"

"Shut up. The less talking we do about it, the less chance we'll be overheard."

Busby had crawled beneath his wagon and was staring up. Effinger and Wilcox finished with the wheels and crawled beneath Wilcox' wagon, tapping axles and undercarriage.

MacIvers said, "Put your guns away, but keep 'em within reach. For God's sake, act unconcerned. Lie down in the shade and at least pretend to sleep."

He got his blankets and spread them on the salt. He laid down and closed his eyes. He tried to relax without success. His nerves and muscles were tight with strain. His ears were tuned to every sound. He wouldn't need his eyes to know if they found anything.

The tapping went on for more than an hour. At last it stopped. After that, he heard the voices of Wilcox and Effinger conversing in low tones, but he couldn't make out their words. Eventually, near midmorning, the camp was still.

But it was a portentous stillness. Nothing had been settled, nothing solved. The seeds of rebellion were still here. All they needed was something to make them grow.

chapter 11

It was a sullen group that hitched up their teams and drove out at sundown. Again, tonight, they left the still carcasses of mules behind.

Three teams to each wagon. That made forty-eight. There were less than two dozen left in the loose herd traveling behind.

MacIvers rode ahead, pushing his floundering horse to the limit of his endurance. He had to know how much farther they had to go. If they were forced to spend another day without hope. . . .

He traveled steadily for more than half the night, sometimes walking and leading his tired horse, sometimes riding. He covered almost twenty miles before he reached the edge of the desert, where thin grass and scrub sagebrush grew.

He turned back immediately. Tomorrow night, if enough mules survived, they would reach this spot.

He rejoined the wagons at dawn. They were circling to form camp. He rode into the center and shouted, "One more night and we'll be out of it. Feed the mules good and give 'em half of the water that's left. Then get yourselves a good sleep. I've seen the edge. We're almost there."

They built fires and cooked breakfast, and afterward they settled down to sleep. There was no searching of the wagons today. There was no bickering. The deep relief everyone felt was evident in the lack of conflict.

And MacIvers slept himself. Soundly, for the first time in many days.

They were up at sundown, cooking, feeding and watering the mules. They hitched up shortly afterward and started out.

Even the mules seemed to know the end was near. They

wallowed ahead. Behind them came the loose herd, numbering hardly more than a dozen.

MacIvers hoped he had not miscalculated the distance, for a disappointment could have serious consequences.

The night dragged on. Gray lightened the eastern sky. All eyes strained ahead through the gloom.

The mules' heads were up, nostrils flaring. Their ears were pricked forward.

Wilcox shouted. He pointed at something up ahead. And suddenly MacIvers saw it too, a break in the endless flatness of the land, a rising of low hills upon which grew scattered brush.

It was not the end. They traveled for several hours more before they reached the spring. But it was the end of the seemingly endless desert. It was the end of the unbearable heat. And it ended, for the time at least, the argument about leaving two of the wagons behind.

MacIvers let them stay at the spring that day and the next, while they refilled water barrels, while the mules grazed and drank their fill, while the women washed clothes, while everyone washed the grime of the desert from their reeking bodies.

He sent Abel on ahead into the Mormon communities to buy more mules. And the wagons ground onward, northeasterly toward Fort Bridger, climbing now, but easily by comparison with the ascent of the Sierras.

At each settlement, Abel met them with mules, and within a week MacIvers' supply of extra mules had been replenished.

Effinger, while still brooding sometimes, stopped trying to incite the others to take over control of the train. He even nodded curtly at MacIvers when he would pass.

Fort Bridger fell behind, and they began the climb toward the divide, warned that the Cheyenne were hostile.

Each settlement they passed along the way had new tales of Indian massacres and atrocities to tell. And now all the men slept with their weapons close at hand. MacIvers posted regular guards at night. He told everyone that no woman was to leave the camp at any time alone.

But on the third night after leaving Fort Bridger the normal noises of the camp were shattered suddenly by Effinger's frantic yell, "Lucy! Lucy!"

A few moments later, Effinger hurried to MacIvers. "Lucy's gone!"

"How long has she been gone?"

"I don't know. Since supper I suppose. I just noticed."

"All right. We'll look around." He turned his head. "Abel, you and Effinger catch horses for the three of us. Coulter, stay here with the others."

66

Abel hurried away. MacIvers said, "Don't worry yet. We're probably not far enough into Indian country to get stirred up. Maybe she—" He had an idea where Lucy was. He glanced over toward the Busby wagon, looking for John. Busby and his wife were there, but John was not.

Effinger hurried away in the direction Abel had gone, and MacIvers walked over to where the Busbys were. "John around?"

"Someplace I guess. I ain't seen him for a while. You think ——"

"I don't think anything. But I know he's been going off with Lucy Effinger sometimes. Don't say anything right now. Effinger's stirred up enough."

Busby nodded. Abel and Effinger returned with the horses, and MacIvers mounted and led out, with the two following along behind.

Beginning fifty yards from camp, MacIvers led them in circles around it, circles that widened steadily. Behind him, Effinger rode in silence.

Half an hour after leaving they came upon John Busby and Lucy, walking toward camp hand in hand.

The three halted. MacIvers said, "I thought you were told not to leave camp."

Busby never got a chance to reply. Effinger slid off his horse and swung a savage, backhanded slap at Busby's face.

MacIvers put his horse between the two. "Effinger, damn you, get back on your horse. Busby, you and Lucy get back to camp."

Busby stood up, rubbing the side of his face. Lucy Effinger began to cry. Effinger tried to get around MacIvers' horse, but MacIvers kept moving the horse and preventing it. John and Lucy ran, still hand in hand, toward camp.

Sullenly Effinger mounted his horse. He growled, "You knew about this."

"I knew. I've seen them together before. What's wrong with it? John Busby's a good steady boy."

"He's trash. He's goddamn poor white trash. I'll—"

They entered the circle of wagons. MacIvers stared at Effinger's angry face disgustedly. He wished he could abandon the Effingers and let them make it alone. He wished he could leave them off someplace and be rid of them.

But he could not. Not unless he could find someone else to drive the wagon in which they were traveling. He'd have to put up with Effinger's troublemaking whether he liked it or not.

Effinger crossed the clearing to Busby's wagon. He looked down. "Trash. Goddamn rebel trash. If I ever catch that boy with my girl again, I'll kill him! You understand?"

Busby stood in front of the fire facing him. John Busby stood beside him, white-faced but straight. His eyes met Effinger's glance steadily. "We're goin' to be married, Mr. Effinger. We was hoping you'd agree."

Effinger's reply was a wordless roar. "The hell! By the Almighty—"

John repeated steadily, "We're still goin' to be married, Mr. Effinger. Whether you agree or not."

Effinger all but fell off his horse. He gained his feet and charged toward the pair. Both John and his father stepped instinctively aside, and Effinger went on, tripped over the fire, and fell with his feet in it.

It might have ended there, MacIvers thought, except that Coulter laughed.

Effinger sat up beyond the fire, beating the smoldering legs of his pants. He got up and charged toward the two Busbys a second time.

Mrs. Busby picked up a heavy pan. She shrieked, "I've seen you fight! You're not going to do my John like you done MacIvers." She swung the pan; it struck Effinger on the back of the head. He sprawled forward, face down.

Across the clearing, Lucy was weeping bitterly. Effinger got to his feet, rubbing the back of his head.

His face was congested with blood. His eyes were furious. MacIvers crossed the clearing hurriedly. Busby's wife was advancing again, the heavy pan held ready for a second blow.

John pleaded, "Ma! Don't! Don't make it worse than it already is."

She turned her head and stared at him uncertainly. Mac-Ivers reached the scene and stood between Effinger and Busby's wife.

Other members of the train were gathering to watch. Some of them were smiling openly at the ludicrousness of the situation. Others were obviously concealing their amusement with difficulty.

Coulter roared, "Let 'em have a go at it, MacIvers. I got five that says she can whip the hell out of him!"

MacIvers hesitated. Effinger had been a troublemaker ever since the journey began. Being beaten by a woman with a heavy pan might well destroy whatever prestige he had with the other travelers. On the other hand, it might make him even more surly and unmanageable.

He glanced at John Busby's face, then at Lucy, weeping almost uncontrollably. He said hoarsely, "Put the pan down, Mrs. Busby. Effinger, you go to your wagon and stay there."

Mrs. Busby lowered the pan. Effinger turned and stalked away furiously, grumbling to himself.

Coulter howled, "What'd you do that for? Why'd you break it up?"

MacIvers didn't bother to reply.

John Busby said, "Thanks, Mr. MacIvers."

He nodded. "Better stay away from Lucy for a while. And don't go out of camp again."

"Yes, sir."

He walked away, glancing toward Effinger's wagon. Lucy was sitting against one of the wagon wheels, her face streaked with tears. Effinger and his wife were arguing bitterly. The two small boys were peeping out from beneath the canvas top, their faces white and scared.

MacIvers couldn't help wondering what would happen if and when this wagon train was attacked. Then he shrugged.

Fires were dying down. One by one, the travelers climbed into their wagons to sleep. MacIvers watched Donna Cory climb into her wagon. She turned her head, caught his glance, and quickly looked away.

He got his blankets out of the wagon. The air was chill tonight, blowing down out of the mountains to the east.

He rolled himself in his blankets. The Effingers were still arguing, but Lucy had disappeared into the wagon.

Brody couldn't have found him a sorrier crew than this, he thought. It was a miracle they'd come this far.

A coyote yipped out on the top of a nearby ridge. Another barked in the canyon up ahead.

MacIvers tensed, but he didn't move. Lucy and John had been very lucky tonight. At least two Indians were out there in the night.

From here to the other side of the mountains and on into the plains beyond, Indians would be watching them. They'd attack if they thought there was any chance of success.

Abel grunted softly from beneath the wagon bed, "You hear what I hear, MacIvers?"

"I heard. Just keep still about it for now. As soon as things quiet down, I'll get up."

He didn't think there was much chance of an attack. But the Indians might try to run off with the mules.

He waited, wide awake, until the camp noises quieted. Then he got up and walked back to where the mules were rope-corralled. He found a spot where he could sit with his back against a rock. And he waited there throughout the night, listening carefully to each small sound.

chapter 12

MacIvers, though he watched the skyline carefully all during the following day, saw no sign of the Indians they had heard the night before.

The pair could have accidentally happened upon the train while out on a hunting party. They might be miles away by now. Or they might be watching yet, intending to follow in the hope of catching someone off alone.

A third alternative occurred to MacIvers. One of the two might have ridden to their village for more warriors. The other might be following.

In any event, there was little he could do. He could post guards at night and be watchful by day. And he could wait.

He rode ahead of the wagons and abandoned the regular order previously maintained by the train. Effinger traveled in the rear, grumbling about the dust. Busby's wagon was at the front. Separated thus, the two families couldn't quarrel.

Strain and weariness was evident in MacIvers, as it was in the others. His face was thinner than it had been before, his mouth more tightly drawn. His eyes were narrowed and his movements quicker than at the journey's start.

He realized that in the next two hundred miles they faced the greatest hazards encountered yet. They had the Rockies to cross. They would be surrounded by hostile plains tribes all the way. The terrain offered countless opportunities for attack.

It angered him to think of the two Indians skulking like coyotes in the darkness. He realized that his anger was personal, even though these were not Comanches. He considered taking Abel and Coulter out to try to find them and get rid of them.

Guiltily he put the thought out of his mind. His first re-

70

sponsibility was to deliver the bullion. Killing a couple of Indians wasn't going to restore his wife to him. Furthermore, if he and the others killed but one, if the other one escaped, the wagons would be in greater danger than before.

As they climbed higher into the mountains, the air took on a new chill. Occasionally MacIvers would see a touch of gold on an aspen's leaves. He admitted the possibility that before they got across the Rockies, they would be hit by an early storm.

They camped that night in a mountain meadow where the grass was thick, where late-blooming wild flowers put a purple cast on the low hillsides, where the stream flattened out to cross this level place.

He put Effinger on one side of the clearing, Busby on the other, with a curt admonition to John to stay away from Lucy Effinger. John nodded respectfully, but there was defiance in his eyes.

MacIvers headed for his own wagon wearily. A fire was going and Coulter was putting coffee on to boil.

MacIvers leaned against the wagon wheel. "Where's Abel?"

"He left awhile ago. Didn't say nothin' to me."

"Hunting, maybe."

"Maybe." Coulter was silent a moment. Then he said, "Abel's a funny one. Since we heard them two Injun bucks last night—"

MacIvers waited and finally said, "Well? What happened since we heard them?"

"He just ain't been the same. He ain't said a word all day. I'd say somethin' to him, and he wouldn't even hear. When we made camp, he got his rifle and walked away."

"Walked? He didn't ride?"

"That's what I said, wasn't it? He walked."

MacIvers frowned. Abel had hunted a lot all along the way. But always on horseback. Never afoot.

He said, "Go ahead and cook supper. I'll be back." He walked to where Peebles was rope-corralling the mules. He caught himself a fresh horse, led him to where he had dumped his gear, and saddled him. He mounted, circled the camp until he picked up the trail left by Abel as he headed through the tall grass toward the stream. He followed it.

The sun was down, but the clouds were flaming from its afterglow. He splashed across the stream and out on the other side. The trail was plain in the high grass, dim where it left the clearing and started up the hill.

Abel must be a fool, he thought. If those two Indians were watching the camp, they'd have seen him leave. They'd have circled ahead and set a trap for him.

71

Yet he knew Abel was not a fool. He scowled. Staring with intent eyes at the trail, occasionally glancing ahead up the steep hillside.

Abel's actions were far from logical in view of what he knew about the man. And yet, he thought, what did he know?

More puzzled than before, he reached the top of the ridge and started into a shallow valley beyond. As he did, he heard a shot, half a mile ahead and slightly to his right. It reverberated back and forth from the surrounding hills. Before it had died away, it was followed by two more.

Light had now faded almost completely from the sky. MacIvers crossed the shallow valley and climbed the ridge beyond.

Reason told him the Indians had set a trap and killed Abel, but he did not believe it. Somehow he knew what he would find.

In a thick grove of pines at the top of the second ridge, he halted suddenly. The only light was that that spread across the land by the slate-gray sky, but it was enough. Enough to see the half-naked Indian spread-eagled on the ground. Enough to see the blood, the work that Abel's savagely vengeful knife had done.

MacIvers hated Indians—all Indians—for what the Comanches had done on his Texas ranch. But not like this. He would never hate like this.

He reined his horse around and headed back toward camp. He found himself hoping Abel had killed both of them.

Abel was squatting beside the fire, staring blankly into it when he arrived. Silently MacIvers dumped his saddle on the ground and loosed his horse in the rope corral. He walked back to the fire thoughtfully. Nothing he could say, nothing he could do, would cool or stop a hatred such as Abel obviously carried in his mind.

He stopped at the fire and stared down. He asked quietly, "Did you get both of them, or only one?"

"Got one. Winged the other." Abel seemed unperturbed.

"Then you know the one you let get away will be back? With maybe thirty or forty more."

Abel nodded. "I'm counting on that, Mr. MacIvers. And when they come I'll get to kill some more."

"I suppose there's a reason for hating them the way you do."

Abel glanced up, his eyes narrowed. "There's a reason."

MacIvers waited. After a moment Abel said, "I came west alone. In fifty-nine. I thought I'd find gold and send for my family later on. I didn't find any gold, so I went on to California and got myself some land. Then I wrote for them to come."

He stared into the fire, his face pale with his memories. He said at last, "They were to come by wagon train and bring our things. Only they didn't come. I waited four months and then started east looking for them. It took me six months to find out what had happened. When I did, all I found was the burned remains of their wagons and some wooden markers."

"How large a family did you have?"

"Four kids. My wife. So don't tell me not to hate Cheyenne, mister. And don't tell me not to kill 'em. You'll just waste that much breath."

MacIvers stared at him a moment more. Vengeance was apparently Abel's sole purpose in life. He didn't care about the Confederate cause. He didn't care if the gold ever reached its destination. Why, then, had he come along?

The answer struck MacIvers with the suddenness of a blow. Gold would buy fighting men and guns. Gold, enough of it, would finance a private campaign against the Cheyenne.

He turned and walked out of the circle of firelight. He stood, surrounded by darkness, staring back at the fires moodily. He was on a fool's errand, he thought, one that could not succeed. He couldn't get eight wagons to their destination by himself.

He clenched his jaws angrily. Perhaps he couldn't. But he could use Abel and Coulter as unscrupulously as they were using him. He could fight the war here as fiercely as he had fought it in the Pennsylvania hills.

He wouldn't revenge himself against the Indians for the death of his wife as Abel was trying to do. But he might justify his absence when she had needed him. Partially at least. Enough so that he could live with himself in peace again.

He returned to the wagons thoughtfully. And he slept, knowing it would be several days before the wounded Indian could bring a war party back.

Day followed day as they wound their monotonous way eastward. Sometimes they followed a stream briefly. Sometimes they followed the trail straight across dry hills or plains. But always, ahead lay the rendezvous MacIvers knew they had with the Cheyenne.

A week after Abel's encounter with the two Cheyenne, MacIvers spotted a lone Indian sitting his horse motionless on a ridge three quarters of a mile away.

Others in the train saw him too. The wagons halted uncertainly.

MacIvers rode to the head of the line. He motioned Effinger on. The bearded man whipped up his mules, and as his wagon rolled ahead, the Indian rode deliberately out of sight.

MacIvers held his horse still as the wagons passed him one by one. When his own wagon came abreast, with Coulter driving, the man yelled, "The son of a bitch! What does he think he's doin', scarin' us?"

MacIvers nodded. "We'll see 'em sitting on the skyline off an' on for several days. They'll get us good and edgy, and then they'll hit. Only they've told us one thing they didn't figure on telling us. There aren't enough of them. They aren't as strong as they'd like to be. If they were, we wouldn't have seen a sign of 'em until they jumped us."

Nevertheless, he posted two guards instead of one. And he roused everyone each morning an hour before first light touched the sky.

Two more days passed. As he had predicted, they saw Indians on the skyline often. Sometimes only one. Sometimes two or three. Once they saw a file of them leisurely crossing a ridge; MacIvers counted twelve.

He frowned worriedly. He might have misinterpreted their motives in deliberately showing themselves, he realized. Instead of trying to make the travelers nervous, they might be trying to lull them into a false sense of superiority.

He would have welcomed the sight of a troop of Union cavalry now. But as far as he knew, the closest cavalry was at Fort Laramie, and that was a long ways off.

The Indians struck about an hour afterward. The wagons were climbing a particularly steep stretch of trail and strung out for nearly a quarter mile. The Indians poured down off the hillsides on both sides, silent until they were less than half a mile away.

MacIvers was riding beside Donna Cory's wagon, about midway in the train. He yanked his revolver from its holster and fired two warning shots into the air.

The lead wagon, Effinger's, made a wide circle, lurching and nearly tipping over as it did. Peebles, behind him, made a similar circle and came racing back. Busby, third in line, stopped.

Donna Cory's teams plunged ahead as MacIvers fired. The wagons behind hers came rattling along behind.

Abel, in the rear with the mules, drove them ahead at a steady run. The Indians were now no more than a quarter mile away.

Loosely grouped, with no time to form a protective circle, the wagons ground to a halt. Locke forgot to set his brake

74

and leaped to the ground, rifle in hand. The frightened mules started up the road.

Cursing Locke's stupidity under his breath, MacIvers spurred his horse after them. He caught up, seized the bridle of the lead mule, and pulled him to a halt. He glanced back, saw the Indians already circling the wagons. Three of them had left the others and were riding toward him, leaning low over their horses' necks.

Guns were firing irregularly, from beneath the wagons, from slits hastily cut in their canvas tops. MacIvers hesitated. He didn't want this wagon burned, and if he left it here, that was what was going to happen to it.

He abandoned his horse suddenly, climbed to the wagon seat, and seized the reins. The long whip cracked out again and again. The mules, already thoroughly frightened, plunged ahead.

MacIvers yanked them around. The wagon tipped precariously.

He straightened them out, and the wagon righted itself. Making a wider circle, he continued the turn, down off the trail and into the shallow gully beneath. Again the whip snaked out.

The Indians were coming straight at him. Two had bows and arrows, the third a gun. An arrow thudded into the canvas top just behind MacIvers. Another buried itself in the hip of one of the mules.

The animal went wild, bucking frantically in the harness, but he was dragged along by the others. The Indians halted just beyond the wagon and whirled their plunging mounts.

MacIvers shifted the reins to his left hand and yanked out his revolver with his right. No need now to drive. The mules were headed back.

An Indian ranged alongside, drawing back his bow, and MacIvers fired instantly.

The arrow snapped from the bow, whistling close over MacIvers' head. The Indian dropped the bow, leaned low over his horse's neck, clinging to his mane. He veered away.

Another fifty yards. MacIvers hauled back on the reins, slowing the teams now so that they wouldn't overshoot. The plunging mules slowed. MacIvers dropped the reins and seized the brake.

He jumped before the wagon was completely halted and struck the ground rolling.

A woman screamed. Hoofs pounded toward MacIvers. He saw an Indian, lance in hand, less than a dozen yards away, coming on with terrifying speed. He froze, muscles gathered and tense, and rolled away at the instant the warrior flung his lance. It buried itself in the ground beside him, penetrating his shirt back and pinning him there helplessly.

Suddenly, as quickly as the Indian had appeared, Donna Cory stood above him, yanking at the lance with both her hands. It came free, and MacIvers sprang to his feet. Pulling her along with him, he ran for the doubtful shelter provided by the hastily halted wagons.

He saw Abel, kneeling beneath a wagon directly behind the great rear wheel. Abel's rifle was rested on one of the spokes, and he was firing and reloading carefully and deliberately. The man's face was without expression, but his eyes gleamed savagely.

MacIvers reached the nearest wagon. Donna fell, and he dropped beside her.

Dust from the galloping Indians' horses rolled over them. The Effingers' two boys were screaming hysterically with fright. Lucy's voice, nearly hysterical too, was trying to quiet them.

Locke was running back and forth aimlessly, unarmed. Sally Bullock was watching him, an expression of utter contempt on her face.

Effinger stood between two wagons, legs spread, head thrown back. His wife crouched at his feet, reloading his rifle. In spite of his dislike of the man, MacIvers felt a stir of admiration. The Busbys and Peebles and his wife were beneath their respective wagons, firing as quickly as they could reload.

He yanked his attention from the others and concentrated on the Cheyenne, now coming around for their third circle of the train.

He moved slightly, so that he could rest his revolver barrel on a wagon spoke. He tried to remember how many loads were left. Two he thought. He had fired twice as a warning when the Indians first appeared. And he had shot the brave from the wagon seat.

He fired deliberately and saw a horse drop to his knees, throwing his painted rider on ahead. The man got up and ran directly toward him, brandishing a tomahawk.

MacIvers sighted carefully a second time. He fired.

The Indian stopped as though he had run into a wall. He stood there, spread-legged, fighting for balance. Then he folded quietly to the ground. He kicked spasmodically and then lay still.

Feeling helpless and naked and exposed, MacIvers began swiftly to reload.

chapter 13

Four Indians lay alone out there, three of them still, one trying to drag a wounded leg as he sought to crawl out of range. The firing had stopped temporarily as the galloping braves swept away and grouped, talking among themselves.

MacIvers finished reloading and looked up just as Abel fired. He glanced around and saw that the wounded Indian was lying still. Beyond, up-country from where they were grouped, lay still another, the one MacIvers had shot from Locke's wagon seat.

He made a quick count of those remaining. Fifteen. He shouted, "Reload your guns! Then get up on your wagon seats and let's get these wagons into a tight circle while we can."

He stepped clear of the wagon and pulled Donna Cory up by the hand. He said, "I'd still be out there if it hadn't been for you."

"Are you hurt?" There was fear in her eyes, but there was also concern.

He shook his head. He left her and walked across to Locke. He said furiously, "Damn you, get yourself a gun and use it."

Locke stared at him dumbly. MacIvers swung an open hand.

It cracked sharply as it struck the side of Locke's face. But it brought some sanity to the man's eyes, and with it, anger. Locke shuffled away. MacIvers turned his head and looked at Sally, settling herself on her wagon seat. He wondered if she'd think it worthwhile to try killing Locke again.

The wagons moved ponderously, falling into line, slowly forming the circle MacIvers had ordered. He holstered his revolver, climbed up on Locke's wagon, and drove it into

77

position himself. He shouted, "Don't unhitch the mules just yet!"

He leaped to the ground as he heard a chorus of high yells from the Cheyenne. Once more they came thundering in, fanned out in a long line this time, heading straight for the wagons, as though they intended to ride straight through.

If they'd done this before . . . but they hadn't, and now the gaps in the circle formed by the wagons were too small to let more than a couple of them through at a time.

Abel's rifle roared and a Cheyenne slid from his saddle, rolling limply as he struck the ground. MacIvers looked around for Donna Cory.

She was climbing down from her wagon seat, looking toward him. And suddenly there was an arrow in her shoulder, its feathered shaft quivering.

He hesitated. Then he got up and ran toward her, turning and firing at a brave less than a dozen yards away.

The brave tumbled from his saddle, but his horse, already pointed toward a gap between two wagons, came plunging through. MacIvers reached Donna and caught her as she fell.

He looked around. One Indian was inside the circle, charging toward him with a stone tomahawk upraised. He tried to bring his gun to bear, but it was too late. The tomahawk came down.

Smoke billowed from the muzzle of Abel's rifle. The Indian was driven sideways out of his saddle, but the horse, unable to turn or stop, struck MacIvers squarely.

He and Donna Cory were flung away helplessly. They crashed against a wagon wheel. Half stunned, MacIvers laid Donna on the ground and pulled himself upright.

All was confusion within the camp. There was blood on Effinger's face. A dead horse lay in the middle of the clearing. The harnessed mules were fighting, plunging, snorting.

Young John Busby was staring at his own bloody arm as though too surprised to believe he really had been hit. Abel was walking toward the Indian who had so nearly killed MacIvers, knife in hand, an insane expression of hatred on his face.

MacIvers crossed to him and struck him squarely on the ear with a fist, then leaped on him and wrenched the knife away.

There was the thunder of hoofs, diminishing as the Indians rode away. MacIvers turned his back on Abel and walked to where Donna Cory lay.

She was conscious, but barely so. Her face was gray and twisted with pain. He knelt over her. "This will hurt, but there's no other way."

78

She nodded wordlessly. He grasped the shaft firmly with both hands and put a knee on her shoulder beside it to hold it down. Then he yanked the arrow out.

It was followed by a rush of blood. Donna's body grew suddenly very limp. He got up, broke the arrow, and flung the pieces away from him. He yelled, "Sally! Come here and bring some bandages."

He walked through the camp. Donna and John Busby were wounded. The blood on Effinger's face was caused by a bullet crease just over his ear. Other than these three, no one was hurt. And there were no dead.

He stared out at the mounted Indians that remained. There were twelve. As he watched, they turned their horses and rode slowly over the crest of a ridge and out of sight.

It was over for the moment. There would be no further attacks today. Yet he knew he did not dare move, did not dare go on. If they were caught strung out again, they might not be so lucky a second time.

He shouted, "We'll camp here tonight. Make a tighter circle with the wagons and corral the mules inside."

Order came slowly out of the shocked confusion within the camp. Effinger's two younger children were sobbing with terror. Lucy, her face white and tear-streaked, was bandaging John Busby's arm.

MacIvers hitched a mule to the dead horse and pulled him out of the circle and beyond for a hundred yards. By the time he returned, the wagons had been pulled into a tighter circle and the travelers were busy unhitching mules.

Donna Cory, her shoulder bandaged but bleeding through the bandage, asked weakly as he stood over her, "Will they come back, or have they gone?"

He said, "I don't know what they'll do. We'll have to wait and see. Indians don't like losing any better than anyone else. If they figure their medicine's bad, they'll leave and we won't see them again. If they figure killing us is worth what they're going to lose, then they'll be back."

She stared up at him, pain in her eyes. But there was something else in her eyes as well. He tried to decide what it was. Dependence, perhaps. Need. He knelt and slid his arms under her. He lifted her and carried her carefully to her wagon. Sally Bullock hurried to him and helped him lift her in. He backed out of the wagon and climbed to the ground, leaving Sally in the wagon to look after her.

He wasn't going to tell Donna or anybody else, but he knew their chances were very poor. Abel's mutilation of the Indian brave had given his friends something to avenge.

Dusk crept almost reluctantly across the land. At last

the exhausted travelers slept, except for MacIvers, Abel, and Effinger, who remained on guard.

Daybreak brought another attack, a howling, slashing raid that was over almost as soon as it began. The only casualties were three mules.

MacIvers smiled grimly as he watched the Indians disappear over the crest of the ridge a second time. They were taking few chances now. Their dead were a grim reminder that the wagon train had a vicious sting.

But, he thought, they didn't have to take chances now. All they had to do was wait. Eventually they'd force the train to move on. Or they'd starve them out. Victory was, for the Cheyenne, only a matter of time.

The days ground on relentlessly, nerve-racking because of the constant vigilance that must be maintained, but monotonous because of enforced inactivity.

Arguments flared, and once more the issue of slavery came up. But in midafternoon of the fourth day, MacIvers heard a distant shout and stared toward the northeast unbelievingly. He saw oxen and the lead wagon of another train roll ponderously around a bend in the canyon. Shortly thereafter he saw the blue uniforms of a cavalry escort.

A jubilant shout went up from the members of the train. Half a dozen mounted cavalrymen detached themselves from the other train and came galloping forward.

The train was a large one, numbering twenty-eight wagons in all. There were fourteen cavalrymen along.

MacIvers, Effinger, and Abel accompanied the lieutenant in charge and his men in a foray against the Cheyenne, but they found the Cheyenne were gone. They followed trail for a dozen miles before they gave up and returned.

There was singing and socializing between the members of the two trains until late that night. But when morning came, the lieutenant and two of his men stopped MacIvers as he was harnessing up his mules.

"I'll have to ask you some questions, Mr. MacIvers."

MacIvers grinned. "You been talking to Effinger?"

The lieutenant looked embarrassed. He nodded. "Effinger thinks you have an ulterior motive in bringing these wagons east."

MacIvers nodded. "He's made that pretty plain. He's another John Brown. And there are some people with us who are from the South."

"You're from the South, aren't you?"

MacIvers nodded. "Texas."

"How does it happen you aren't in uniform?"

80

MacIvers said, "Lieutenant, there are thousands of men in the South who aren't in uniform, just as there are thousands of men in the North."

"I'll have to search your wagons anyway."

MacIvers shrugged. "They were searched in California. They've been searched by Effinger and Wilcox. Once more won't hurt."

He watched the embarrassed lieutenant walk away. He watched the halfhearted search. When it was finished, he waved his wagons on.

They ground upward toward South Pass, staying closer together now. Abel drove Donna Cory's wagon, but John Busby insisted on driving the mules as before, in spite of his wounded arm.

Donna spent a great deal of time sleeping in her wagon, but occasionally she would walk beside it. And sometimes she would ride up on the seat. Her arm healed, but slowly, because the arrow had infected it.

They reached South Pass in mid-September and started down the other side. They covered the worst grades without incident.

It happened as unexpectedly as had the Indian attack. To MacIvers' wagon, which Coulter drove.

MacIvers was ahead of it, and the grade was long and steep. One after another of the wagons negotiated it, using only the brakes to hold them back.

But the wagon Coulter was driving rolled suddenly ahead, gaining speed, crowding the mules, and forcing them into a run. Coulter stood on the seat, fighting the brake as Locke had done earlier. MacIvers got a glimpse of his frightened face and saw him shout. It was an instant before the words reached him, so great was the distance between them. "The brake. Somethin's wrong."

MacIvers whirled his horse, but he knew there was nothing he could do. He watched Coulter abandon his efforts to set the brake and drive. The wagon, gaining speed steadily until it seemed as though it would overrun the mules, roared down the road, lurching from side to side, skidding around the gentle turns.

Coulter would be killed if he didn't jump. The speed of the wagon was terrifying, the racket it made equally so. It roared past the wagon in front of it, clearing it by no more than half a foot.

The mules were running as MacIvers had never seen them run before. The wagon roared around a turn slightly sharper than the rest.

For an instant MacIvers thought it had made it. Then he saw it begin to skid. A wheel went over the edge.

Then it was rolling, splintering as it rolled, and the six mules were a fighting, bleeding tangle of harness and flying hoofs. A column of dust rose fifty feet in the air. Coulter was nowhere to be seen.

The other men left their wagons and started running toward the wreck. MacIvers stood in his stirrups and roared, "Stay with your wagons, damn you! You want to wreck some more?"

He galloped his horse toward the column of rising dust. Coulter was picking himself up from the slope, fifty feet short of the wreck. He limped slightly, but shook his head when MacIvers asked him if he was hurt. He followed MacIvers down the slope.

The gold was the first thing MacIvers saw. Gleaming in the sun, the bars lay scattered over an area extending fifty feet above the wreck. They'd spilled from the wagon like beans from a ruptured sack.

MacIvers began to pick them up and toss them beneath the wrecked wagon. He glanced over his shoulder and up the slope.

Effinger stood at the edge of the trail looking down. He bawled, "What?" Then he was running down the slope, taking great long strides because of the steepness of the grade. He stooped and picked up one of the bars.

He turned an outraged face toward MacIvers. "I knew—damn you, I knew there was something."

He was carrying a rifle, something no man had let himself be caught without since the Indian attack earlier. He raised it, muzzle pointing at MacIvers' chest.

MacIvers snatched out his revolver. He fired instantly, but into the ground at Effinger's feet. "Hold it! Drop that damn rifle, or I'll blow your head off!"

Effinger hesitated.

Coulter's voice, equally sharp, yelled, "Drop it, he said!"

The rifle clattered to the ground at Effinger's feet. Coulter said, "Kill him, MacIvers. Kill him before he spills the beans."

MacIvers hesitated for the briefest moment. Killing a man in cold blood went against his grain, but he knew it had to be done. He raised his gun.

He froze as another shout came to him from above. Looking up, he saw Wilcox and Busby standing where Effinger had stood only moments before.

Effinger's face was white and thoroughly scared.

MacIvers said, "Coulter, go get Abel to drive Mrs. Cory's wagon down here. We'll load these bars."

Coulter began to climb the slope. Effinger looked around as if he'd like to run.

MacIvers said sharply, "Stay where you are."

Effinger stared at him defiantly, "You can't—you don't dare—"

MacIvers' eyes were cold. "Mister, the war's right here. I can do anything I have to do. So keep that big mouth shut and stand real still."

Effinger closed his mouth like a trap. He watched MacIvers nervously.

Wilcox and Busby were climbing down toward them. Coulter reached the pair. He said something to them that MacIvers didn't hear. He pointed his gun at them and followed them back up the slope.

This was the thing MacIvers had dreaded all the way from California. There would be no hiding it from the members of the train. There would be no hiding it if the train encountered Union cavalry again.

Several hundred miles still lay ahead, between here and the safety of the Southern border states. How he was going to make it now, MacIvers didn't know. He had a sudden, bleak certainty that he wasn't going to make it at all. He was going to lose the gold and be hanged as a traitor for his pains.

But it hadn't happened yet. And until it did, he intended to go on. There had to be a way of getting through.

chapter 14

For a time there was only silence from above. Then MacIvers heard the rattle of a wagon and saw Abel driving Donna Cory's wagon across the hillside toward him. It was tilted precariously, but Abel drove it expertly. When it reached him, he motioned the man to drive it into position below the wreck.

The hurt mules were still kicking and fighting. MacIvers said, "Cut 'em loose. Shoot the ones you have to. Then let's load these bars."

Abel climbed down off the wagon seat, drew his knife, and began to hack the hurt mules loose. Two got up and ran on down the slope. One was already dead. The other three had broken legs; Abel shot them one by one.

MacIvers said, "Effinger, start tossing up these bars."

The man glowered at him for an instant. Meekly then, he began to pass bars of gold to Abel, who had climbed into the wagon again.

MacIvers watched, his gun still in his hand. When Effinger had finished, he motioned for Abel to drive the wagon away.

He picked up Effinger's rifle, walked to where his horse was standing, and mounted. He said, "Go back to your wagon. But keep one thing in mind. I'll be hanged if I'm caught, and you can't hang a man more than once."

For once Effinger was silent. He trudged up the slope, and when he reached the trail, he headed toward his wagon. He climbed to the seat silently.

MacIvers stared at the seven remaining wagons as they formed a line and rolled ponderously down the trail. He didn't know whether Busby and Wilcox had seen the gold or not. He did know both of them must realize something was wrong.

Effinger wouldn't have a chance to talk to anyone today, but tonight. . . .

MacIvers knew how impossible it would be to keep something like this from spreading throughout the train. For a moment he considered disarming everyone. He discarded the idea almost at once. They were still in Indian country, and they had a long way to go before they'd be out of it. If only he, Coulter, and Abel had guns, they wouldn't have much chance if Indians attacked the train again.

Donna Cory was riding on the seat beside Sally Bullock. She looked at him strangely as he passed. She would know soon, he thought, that he had used and deceived her. She had said she would hate him for that. He shrugged wearily to himself. Before this was finished, he would be thoroughly hated by everyone in the wagon train.

Down and down they went, emerging at last upon the rolling plain. Now the trail turned east, toward Fort Laramie on the Platte.

Tension was unmistakable among the members of the train. They looked at MacIvers from their wagon seats, fully aware that something was wrong, not yet knowing what it was.

The sun sank toward the mountain range behind the train. At last, near dusk, MacIvers motioned for the lead wagon to turn and start forming a protective circle for the night.

Scarcely had they begun the circle than Effinger roared at Wilcox, "There's bullion hidden in these wagons, Ned. Gold bullion for the South!"

MacIvers glanced at Donna Cory. Her face was still pale from her wound, but her eyes were angry and filled with disillusionment. He rode up beside Sally Bullock's wagon and stared at Donna, holding her glance with the sheer force of his own. He said, "It's true. The gold is for the Confederacy. I'm a captain of Confederate cavalry."

When she didn't reply, he said almost irritably, "I'm a soldier, ma'am. I'm doing what I believe to be right."

Still she didn't speak. He stared at her a moment more, then turned his horse and rode away.

The circle was formed. Effinger and Wilcox stood near the endgate of Effinger's wagon, talking in undertones.

MacIvers rode to the center of the circle. "All right. Now you know. There is an equal amount of gold in each wagon, and it's all going to the Confederacy."

He let the babel of voices die away before he went on,

"I'll give you fair warning. Nothing is going to stop these wagons from reaching their destination. The war is here, as of right now. You will do as you are told. Whoever refuses will be shot."

No voices now. Only their faces and their eyes, studying him, evaluating what he had said.

He rode out of the circle, dismounted, and unsaddled his horse. He put the animal with the mules, then walked back toward the camp.

Fort Laramie lay ahead, yet he knew he didn't dare go near the place. He also realized he could no longer travel the regular trail. He would have to cut across country and hope he ran into no roving cavalry patrols. He was glad that all the frontier garrisons were undermanned.

He headed toward the fire Abel and Coulter had built. Peebles caught at his sleeve as he passed. "I'm with you, cap'n. I'm with you all the way."

He grunted, "Good," and went on. Peebles and Busby both were from the South. He could expect their support, such as it was. He stared across the clearing at Effinger and Wilcox. Those two were the strong ones. Those two were the ones to watch. Already they were planning something.

Abel muttered, "You'd better get their guns. That damn Effinger might do anything."

"We're still in Indian country. And there are only two of them."

Abel shrugged and returned his attention to the fire. Mac-Ivers watched him, then watched Coulter, who was endlessly whetting his knife. These two were more dangerous to him than Effinger and Wilcox could ever be.

He began to think of all the ways Effinger and Wilcox could stop the train from getting through. They could drive off the mules. They could disable or burn the wagons. Their efforts did not have to be violent to be successful.

MacIvers said, "Maybe we'd better get their guns at that. Abel, circle around and come on them from behind. Coulter, come with me."

He started across the clearing toward the whispering pair. Effinger glanced up. He lunged for his wagon, reached inside, and seized a revolver that was hidden there. Wilcox already had a rifle in his hand.

Effinger bawled, "Lucy! Mary! Take the kids and run!"

The other members of the train stopped what they were doing and stared. No one made a move to intervene. Abel began to run.

Effinger snapped a shot at him. Abel dived beneath a

nearby wagon. He poked his gun out from behind a wheel.

MacIvers roared, "No! Let 'em go!"

Beside him Coulter grumbled, "You goddamned fool!"

MacIvers stopped. He watched Effinger and Wilcox disappear into the darkness beyond the circle of wagons, herding their wives and Effinger's children ahead of them.

Abel crawled from beneath the wagon and crossed the circle to him. "What'd you stop me for?"

MacIvers didn't reply because he knew his answer wouldn't make sense to either of them. He was a soldier, not a murderer, and if he hadn't stopped Abel, it would have been murder. He grunted, "They can't go far. They've got no food. We'll find 'em in the morning and bring 'em back."

He swung around and returned to the fire. John Busby was watching him from nearby, a worried, scared expression on his face. After hesitating several moments, young Busby crossed the clearing to him. "What's going to happen, Mr. MacIvers? You're not going to leave them, are you?"

MacIvers shook his head. "I'm not going to leave them."

"Can I go out and talk to Lucy? I——"

MacIvers shook his head. "You stay here. Effinger's liable to shoot you before he realizes who you are."

The boy hesitated, swallowed a couple of times, and finally said, "I'll help you, Mr. MacIvers. But not against Lucy or Lucy's folks."

"All right, John." He watched the boy return to his father's fire. It suddenly seemed unbelievable that people so close in other ways should be split apart so violently by their ideas and beliefs. He got himself a plate of venison stew from the pot over the fire. He didn't particularly want to eat, but he ate anyway. Afterward, he circled the camp outside the wagons, staring into the night and listening.

Finding and disarming Effinger and Wilcox wasn't going to be as simple as he had made it sound. Effinger was a man of staunch convictions, who had more than once proved his readiness to fight for them. If he chose to fight this time. . . .

MacIvers frowned. More than five hundred miles still remained; even if they managed to cover twenty miles a day, it would be nearly a month before he reached safety with the gold. A gunfight between members of the train was certain to decimate their number and reduce their chances of getting through.

The fires inside the circle of wagons died to glowing coals. Some of the people sought their beds. Others sat uneasily, guns in their hands or nearby, staring into the darkness.

MacIvers returned to his own fire. He said, "You two get some sleep. I'll watch until midnight. Then I'll call you."

Coulter and Abel nodded, got their blankets, and rolled up in them. Coulter began to snore almost immediately.

MacIvers leaned against a wagon wheel and stared at the fire moodily. He wondered how many of the group would be dead by this time tomorrow. If only a fight could be avoided. . . .

But he knew it could not. He didn't dare leave Effinger and Wilcox out here alone, this close to Fort Laramie.

Endlessly the night dragged on. At midnight, he wakened Abel and Coulter. But even though he wrapped himself in his blankets and laid down on the ground, he couldn't sleep. All he could think was that tomorrow he would be fighting not only Effinger and Wilcox, but their families too—unless he could figure out some way. He slept at last and did not awaken until dawn began to gray the sky.

There was an ominous stillness in the camp. People went about cooking breakfast and stowing their wagons in silence. Occasionally MacIvers would catch one of them glancing at him furtively and uneasily. When all was ready, he mounted his horse and yelled, "Get going. Abel, drive Effinger's wagon and lead out. John, you take Wilcox' wagon. Sally Bullock can drive her own, and Coulter, you take Mrs. Cory's."

Coulter growled, "What are we going to do about that bunch out there?"

"Nothing right away. If they don't show themselves, you and I and Abel will ride back and find them later on today."

Coulter grumbled something disapprovingly. He climbed to the seat of Donna Cory's wagon and picked up the reins.

The train moved out, heading east once more. MacIvers positioned himself in the center of it. He was fairly sure that Effinger and Wilcox had placed themselves on the trail ahead. He was also fairly sure that neither man would shoot without first calling out.

A quarter mile passed. Up ahead, MacIvers saw a place where the trail crossed a wash. It would happen there, he thought. He glanced back at the spare mules. They were following the trail docilely, grazing as they came. They had been herded in the wake of the train so long that following had become second nature with them.

The first wagon rolled down into the wash.

He had sent Abel in that first wagon for a reason. He knew Abel would not be taken by surprise.

And he had been right. Even before the first shot sounded hollowly from the bottom of the wash, he saw Abel abandon his wagon seat in a single flying leap. The man rolled on the ground, gun in hand.

MacIvers bawled, "Coulter! Set your brake and come on!"

Others were jumping down off their wagon seats. The two Busbys. Peebles, Donna Cory and Sally Bullock remained where they were. So did Locke.

MacIvers galloped to the edge of the wash. He reached it just as Abel opened fire from behind his forward wagon wheel.

MacIvers' gun was in his hand. He stared down into the wash.

Effinger's convictions might be strong, but his strategy wasn't. He and Wilcox lay behind a hastily erected barricade of brush and dirt. Behind them their wives huddled against the dirt bank of the wash. Lucy was a bit farther on, an arm around each of the terrified boys.

MacIvers yelled, "Effinger! Wilcox! Throw down your guns!"

A bullet from Abel's gun showered dirt from the bank above the pair. It ricocheted and whined away into space.

MacIvers yelled, frantically this time, "Damn it, throw down your guns!"

Effinger leaped to his feet. His bearded face turned upward. Behind MacIvers, the two Busbys and Peebles appeared. Effinger's face was red with fury. His eyes glowed fiercely, MacIvers roared, "Your families! They're in the line of fire."

Effinger turned his head and stared toward Abel down the wash. He turned around and stared back at where his family was. He realized that what MacIvers said was true. But he didn't act quickly enough. He didn't drop his gun. He just stood there, helplessly hesitating.

Abel's gun barked once more. And MacIvers heard the flat, unmistakable sound of a bullet striking flesh.

Effinger was still standing, apparently unhurt. Wilcox, down behind the barricade, also seemed to be unhurt.

MacIvers' chest felt hollow and cold. He turned his head almost reluctantly and heard a sudden, terrible scream.

Mrs. Effinger began to run. Back toward Lucy and the boys. Back to where Lucy's body was rolling limply down the last few feet of bank into the sandy bottom of the wash.

Effinger dropped his gun. Wilcox stood up, hands raised above his head, a gray, shocked expression on his face. Abel came walking up the wash and took his gun from him. He picked up Effinger's just as the man began to shamble in the direction of his family.

Mrs. Effinger reached Lucy. Weeping hysterically, she knelt and cradled Lucy's head in her lap.

Abel stood frozen, staring, shocked by the realization that only his bullet could have struck Lucy where she stood.

Effinger reached the girl. He said brokenly, "Lucy! You hurt? Where are you hurt? Answer me! Lucy! Answer me!"

Effinger's wife looked up, tears running down her cheeks. Her voice was hollow. "She can't answer you. God forgive you, your daughter's dead."

MacIvers heard a choked sound beside him. He glanced down at John Busby. The boy's mouth was trembling. His eyes were filled with tears. He leaped off the edge and plunged down the bank. He reached the Effingers. He stopped, staring down, weeping uncontrollably.

Effinger turned his head and looked blankly at him. There was a stony calm about Effinger's expression, but his eyes were like those of a wounded animal. He lifted his glance and stared at MacIvers accusingly.

MacIvers turned his head. "Busby, you and Peebles get shovels. Start a grave."

He heard them move away. Effinger was still looking at him as if he were a murderer.

Suddenly he hated himself, hated this job he had taken on. He hated Abel for firing the fatal shot. But mostly, he found himself hating Effinger. For blaming him when the blame rested squarely with the man himself.

Yet his voice was strangely gentle when it came. "John, pick her up and carry her up here."

Lucy Effinger was dead, a casualty of the war between the states just as surely as if she had been a soldier on the battlefield. And nothing any of them could do would bring her back.

chapter 15

It was a somber group that gathered at Lucy Effinger's grave.

Peebles and Busby had dug it on a small knoll overlooking the trail. Below, the wagons waited while the group filed up the hill. Busby and Peebles carried Lucy's body, swathed in a blanket, and laid it gently down beside the grave.

MacIvers, Abel, and Coulter stood back about fifty feet away and listened to Effinger's grief-stricken voice as he read from the Bible in his hands.

The silences as he paused in his reading were broken by the women's sobs. John Busby stood, white-faced and silent, staring at Effinger's bearded face.

When the service was over, Lucy's body was slowly lowered into the grave with ropes. Peebles pulled up the ropes, and Busby began to fill in the grave. Young Busby broke and ran, sobbing, toward the wagons down below.

The rest of the people trooped slowly down the hill. MacIvers met them. "We've got a couple of things to do. I want all the guns. This isn't going to happen a second time."

Nobody spoke.

He continued, "When that's done, I want each of you to shift the load in your wagon and rip up the floor. We'll put all the gold in two wagons."

He couldn't help glancing at Donna Cory's face. She was watching him but her expression was unreadable. She almost seemed stunned. He stood aside and watched them walk on toward their wagons. He watched as they meekly took out their guns and passed them to Abel and to Coulter on the ground. They began to shift the loads in the wagons so that they could get at the false floors underneath.

Since Donna Cory's wagon and that of Jack Locke were loaded more lightly than the others, he ordered the gold loaded into those two. He put Effinger and Locke in one of them, Wilcox and Peebles in the other. The two Busbys worked on the ground, taking bars passed to them by Coulter and Abel and handing them up.

MacIvers rode eastward along the trail for several miles until he reached a high point from which he could see for miles ahead. He saw no dust, no sign of either wagon train or cavalry. Relieved, he returned. At least they weren't going to be surprised.

The gold was still being transferred when he returned, but the job was almost done. He watched coldly.

Sally Bullock came to him and stared up. She gestured with her head toward Locke. "Why couldn't it have been him? Why did it have to be Lucy, who never hurt anyone?"

"I don't know."

Abel yelled, "That's all of it!"

MacIvers nodded. "You and Coulter get up on the two wagons that are carrying the gold. Stow things so that the bars aren't going to be shifting all the time. The rest of you get ready to roll. We'll pull off the main trail four or five miles. Then we'll camp. We'll go on after dark."

Half an hour later the wagons turned off the trail and headed south. Abel drove the lead wagon, Coulter the second in line. After Coulter came Sally and Donna, in Sally's wagon.

Locke, whose wagon was one of those commandeered to carry bullion, rode a horse at the rear, driving the mules along. Busby's wagon followed Sally's, and Peebles' was fifth in line. Wilcox and Effinger drove the last two.

In a small depression, hidden from the main trail running to the north, MacIvers halted the train. He allowed no fires to be built.

Each of his orders was met with sullenness. Locke sought out Abel and Coulter, making himself agreeable. Busby and Peebles sat together, talking in low tones.

MacIvers wondered if they realized how easy they were making it for him to read their motives and their thoughts. Busby and Peebles had never been close before. It was therefore apparent that both were wondering if it would not be possible to get their hands on a few bars of the gold.

Locke was trying to make a deal with Coulter and Abel.

And Effinger watched MacIvers with smoldering eyes whenever MacIvers was near. His thoughts were obvious. Unable to live with his own guilt because of his daughter's death, he was blaming MacIvers for it. He'd kill if he could, any way he could.

The afternoon dragged on. At sundown, MacIvers ordered

them on, rearranging the order of the train so that Wilcox and Effinger were sandwiched between Abel and Coulter up in front.

He rode ahead to scout a trail, pushing his horse hard, returning often to tell Abel which way was easiest. He avoided deep washes across which there were no easy routes. He circled buttes. But he tried to keep the direction always east and slightly south.

In the daytime the furtive plotting went on. Between Coulter and Abel and Locke. Between Busby and Peebles. Between Wilcox and Effinger. And MacIvers, feeling more alone than ever before in his life, waited and watched.

Miles rolled behind, almost twenty every night. And days passed with a monotony that threatened to lull MacIvers' watchfulness. He grew nervous and irritable from lack of sleep. But the closer they got to the Missouri, the more watchful he became. He had a feeling—one that grew until it became almost an obsession with him. The various groups within the train were watching him for signs that he had reached the point where exhaustion would incapacitate him. He became afraid to sleep. And when he did sleep, it was to doze with his gun in his hand, or sometimes to dismount at night and sleep, his horse's reins looped securely around his wrist, until the wagons caught up with him.

Donna Cory watched him whenever he was near. It seemed to him that of all the people in the wagon train, her face held less dislike, less condemnation.

The time came, as he had known it must, when he could no longer stay awake, when he could no longer simply doze. He slept, deeply, for the first time in many days.

He awoke with a start. Someone was shaking him violently. He sat up and stared around groggily.

Effinger was less than fifteen feet away, a singletree held in both hands like a club. Donna Cory knelt beside him, shaking him, crying frantically at him to wake up.

Effinger stopped when he saw that MacIvers was awake. MacIvers raised his gun, but he didn't speak.

Effinger stared at him for a moment with smoldering, hating eyes. Then he turned and stalked away.

MacIvers rubbed his eyes and licked his lips. He looked at Donna steadily. "That's the second time you've saved my neck. I thought——"

"I may not agree with you, but I'm not going to stand by while someone splits your head open."

He studied her, watching the flush that crept into her face under his steady scrutiny. Once more he felt a hunger, a need for her, and it showed plainly in his eyes.

She started to get up, but he caught her hand. "No. Don't go yet."

She settled back reluctantly. It was late afternoon. The sky was overcast and the air was cool.

He felt incredibly dirty, and his beard was almost two weeks old. He said harshly, "A soldier doesn't choose his assignments. You must know that."

"But why did it have to be you? Why?"

"Maybe they knew what was driving me. I went into the Confederate army because I believed it was right. Then, when my wife was killed—well, I couldn't help feeling that if I hadn't gone, she would still be alive. I knew if the South lost, my going would have been useless and unnecessary. Her death would have been a waste. I'd be to blame.

"Maybe I fought harder because of it. Maybe they felt I'd try harder than anyone else to get this gold through. Or maybe they just knew I was familiar with wagons and mules and with the terrain out here."

He was silent for a time, trying to bring some order out of the confusion in his mind.

She said, "Your two friends aren't here for the same reasons you are."

"No. Both of them want the gold for themselves. Coulter, because he's greedy. Abel, because he hates the Indians and wants to equip an expedition against them."

She was frowning. Her eyes were troubled. "I hate what you're doing. I hate to think of this gold reaching the Confederacy because I know it will be used to buy more guns. And more Union soldiers like my husband will be killed."

He managed to smile faintly. "Then you're against me too?"

She shook her head. "Not against you. Against what you're doing, perhaps, but not against you."

He said, "You know there's not much chance of getting through, don't you? Kansas is Union, and there are settlements. All Effinger or Wilcox would have to do would be to get to one of them. I'd have Union cavalry on top of me before I knew what was happening."

"What will happen to you if you're caught?"

He grinned ruefully. "Depends on who catches me, I guess. These Kansas hotheads would probably hang me. Effinger would like that. If it's the Army that catches me, I'll either be shot or put in a prison camp until the end of the war."

"Can't you avoid the settlements?"

"For a while I can. We haven't reached them yet. I think if I could get just one whole day's sleep——"

She murmured, "You can. Tomorrow. I'll stay awake and watch."

94

For an instant his eyes locked with hers. It was Donna who looked away, flushed and uncomfortable. He said, "That won't make you very popular."

"I don't care about that." She avoided his glance. There was a current running between them that both could feel. He put out a hand and covered hers.

She got to her feet suddenly. She hurried away without looking back.

She wanted him as much as he wanted her, he realized. But there could be no future in it. Even if he did get through, which seemed unlikely at the moment, he'd be going back to the Army of the Confederacy. She'd be going north. They'd never see each other again.

Glancing up, he saw Sally Bullock watching him. Her expression was forlorn, as though she had seen something she wanted desperately, but could never have. She looked away instantly.

MacIvers got up stiffly. He stared at Coulter and at Abel. He glanced toward Busby and Peebles, talking in low tones near Busby's wagon. Effinger was squatting before a fire, staring moodily into it.

He could dismiss Busby and Peebles as threats, he supposed. They'd do nothing violent. They'd steal if they could, but they wouldn't risk their lives.

Coulter hated him and would kill him if he could. Abel would do whatever was necessary to get away with the gold.

Effinger was, he guessed, the worst of all of them. Effinger was filled with what he thought was righteous wrath. He'd kill, and afterward he'd convince himself it was the will of God.

Coulter, Abel, and Effinger. He'd watch those three. And hope he hadn't underestimated the others.

He dipped out some water from the half-empty barrel on the lead wagon and washed. He got out his razor and scraped the whiskers from his face. Then he walked to where the mules were rope-corralled and caught his horse. He saddled and rode out toward the east to scout trail for tonight.

chapter 16

On the following day MacIvers slept deeply and without interruption while Donna Cory sat nearby. He awoke about five, feeling more rested than he had for weeks.

She had supper ready for him, and he ate hungrily. Staring across the circle as he ate, he noticed that Busby had joined Coulter and Abel and Locke. Peebles sat beside his own fire with his wife.

Tonight, he thought, he would turn straight south. They still had more than a hundred miles to go before reaching the settlements but he knew he should stay far enough away so that neither Effinger nor Wilcox would attempt reaching them.

At dusk, the wagons rolled south, led by Abel as usual. MacIvers rode ahead to scout the trail.

He frowned slightly as he rode, puzzled at his own uneasiness. He tried to reason it away without very much success. It could be caused by suddenly feeling rested after being so very tired. Or by Busby unexpectedly adding himself to the Abel-Coulter-Locke camp. Or simply by the overcast that had earlier hidden the sun and that now completely hid the stars.

The air felt damp, and it was cooler than it had been. At midnight it began to rain.

MacIvers turned his horse and returned the way he had come. Distant thunder rolled across the sky. Occasionally lightning flashed.

As he rode, his uneasiness increased. He spurred his horse into a steady trot.

Rain fell harder now, slanting sharply out of the northeast on a rising wind. Lightning flashed more frequently in the direction he was heading, and thunder became an almost continuous rumble in the skies.

The center of the storm was ahead. It had probably enveloped the wagons already, turning the ground underfoot to mud, filling the dry washes that cut raggedly across the plain. He urged his horse into a rolling lope, maintaining it as long as he dared. Tension mounted steadily in him.

He was so close, so close to his destination. Perhaps that explained his uneasiness, he thought. He could see the end, yet he knew that before he reached it, he would face a greater threat then any encountered so far.

He was soaked to the skin. Rain ran from the brim of his hat and was blown back into his face. He began to chill and to shiver violently.

The wagons had probably stopped, he thought, to wait out the worst fury of the storm. His horse slipped and almost fell. MacIvers reluctantly slowed him to a trot.

He reached a wide wash and halted at its edge. He could hear the low roar of water and could occasionally see the flood as lightning illuminated the sky.

He forced his horse into it, surprised to find it so deep that the animal was forced to swim. The water was like ice, and its surface was speckled with floating hail.

The horse climbed out on the other side and shook himself. MacIvers urged him on. He should be meeting the wagons soon.

Another mile fell behind. And suddenly, in a particularly bright lightning flash, he saw them ahead of him.

They were halted, as he had expected them to be, but they had not formed a circle. Two were separated from the others, separated by a wide, normally dry wash like the one he had so recently crossed. Separated by a flood of roaring water and floating hail.

Lightning flashed again. Thunder crackled almost immediately. And something else flashed from the lead wagon on this side of the wash. The report was almost lost in the crackle of thunder from above.

MacIvers' horse stumbled, then whirled and began to buck. The gun flashed again. This time the report was plain and sharp in the momentary lull between thunderclaps.

Brutally MacIvers yanked up his horse's head. Savagely he sank his spurs. The animal stopped bucking and ran recklessly, sliding in the ooze underfoot. He traveled for about fifty yards. Then he stumbled again. His forelegs went down. He somersaulted onto his back, throwing his rider clear.

MacIvers landed, sliding, at the very edge of the roaring

wash. He struggled to his feet, grateful for the darkness, grateful that, for now at least, no lightning flashed.

His gun was gone; it had slipped from his holster when he fell. He groped for it helplessly, fury growing in his mind.

Abel and Coulter had planned well, he thought, and had taken advantage of the unexpectedness of the storm. They had crossed the wash while it was still fordable, but had halted on the other side, no doubt feigning trouble, thus preventing the others from crossing. Now a crossing for the others was impossible.

He heard footsteps approaching him in the mud. Each one made a sucking sound. Lightning flashed, showing him a man, unrecognizable, coming warily toward him, revolver ready in his hand.

He found his gun as darkness again enveloped the streaming land. He got to his feet and plunged away. Damn! The gun barrel was probably filled with mud. He didn't dare fire until he had cleared it.

Flame spat wickedly at him, probing, searching. Bullets made wet, smacking sounds as they churned into the mud at his feet.

He broke into a run, weaving back and forth as he ran. Behind him, his pursuer also began to run.

MacIvers circled gradually until he was headed directly back toward the wagons. He stuck the revolver muzzle into his mouth and blew. It was stopped with mud all right. And with his hands covered with mud, forced to remain moving, in complete darkness, it was impossible to clear it now. He shook the gun violently and tried again. This time a small amount of air went through.

Perhaps it would fire when the need for it came. Perhaps it would fire without blowing up in his face. But he didn't dare risk it unless there was no other choice.

Across the wash, as the lightning flashed again, he saw Locke and Busby standing together on the bank. They had conspired with Abel and Coulter for a share in the gold, and perhaps Abel and Coulter would have used them if there had been need for it. But now fifty feet of rushing water stood between the two and the loot they hoped to share.

The two wagons were now less than a dozen yards away. Another gun spat at him from the seat of the second one.

He veered aside, putting the first between him and this second gun. Lightning flashed and the gun behind him roared.

But he saw something else in that brief flash of light. He saw Locke plunge into the wash, as though to wade across. He disappeared instantly. His cry was lost as the water closed over his head. The flash died as MacIvers reached the nearest wagon and dived under it.

Frightened by gunfire, by the lightning and thunder, and by the sight of MacIvers plunging past, the mules began to move, straining, lunging in the mud. Though the brake was locked, the wagon began to slide.

MacIvers turned around and scrambled along, trying to stay beneath it, trying to avoid being left in the open, without cover or protection from the gun on the second wagon's seat. He saw the legs of a man beside the wagon. And he knew suddenly that he was caught, with a gun he dared not fire except as a last resort, with no place to go.

He lunged from beneath the wagon, feet and knees sliding in the mud, and threw his body against the legs immediately beside the sliding wagon. The man went down with a high yell of surprise.

MacIvers plunged on, praying soundlessly that no lightning would illuminate him for another few seconds at least.

From the seat of the second wagon, Coulter yelled, "Abel! Damn it, sing out! Where is he now?"

The answering shout from Abel was unintelligible. Suddenly, from across the wash, a rifle opened up. The shots were widely spaced, allowing time for reloading between each one.

Coulter bellowed, "Where the hell did that gun come from? I thought we had 'em all!"

MacIvers stopped running fifty feet from the two wagons. He fumbled with his gun, shaking it again.

This time the muzzle cleared, perhaps from the steadily pouring rain that had undoubtedly helped to wash it out.

He could hear Coulter and Abel talking among themselves, but he couldn't make out their words.

The lightning and thunder was moving south. The flashes were not so bright, but in one of them, Abel yelled, "There! Over there!"

Instantly both Abel's and Coulter's guns flashed. Just before he heard the reports, MacIvers felt a burning blow on his right thigh. He was hit, he thought as he fell.

Coulter yipped, "I got the son of a bitch! I got him!"

They broke and ran toward him, like hunters who have downed a deer. MacIvers began to curse under his breath, fiercely and angrily. He was hit, but he wasn't going to lie here and let them murder him.

He stuffed the revolver in his belt. Using both hands, he raised himself enough to get his good leg under him. With a sudden effort he forced himself to his feet.

They were now less than twenty-five feet away, coming on about ten feet apart. They were approaching cautiously even though MacIvers still had not fired a shot.

If lightning flashed right now, they'd cut him down from two sides. But it stayed dark, for a few moments at least.

MacIvers tried the leg. He could feel the warmth of blood coursing down his thigh. He could feel a certain numbness, but no great amount of pain, as he put his weight on it. He took a step, another, a third.

He couldn't run. But as slowly as they were approaching, at least he need not be where they expected him to be.

He walked straight toward the roaring, bank-filled wash. The rifle across it was silent now. He turned, his back to the wash, and faced the pair.

As though at a signal, lightning illuminated the sky. He fired and saw the two wheel, crouch, and fire at him almost simultaneously.

He could distinguish between them now. Coulter was on his right, Abel on his left. He had fired at Coulter, and he saw the man go down.

But he was also hit himself. He felt himself driven back as though by the savage kick of a mule. He was falling, and he felt the icy water in the wash close above his head.

He fought instinctively to surface, to bring his head up out of the water so that he could gulp the life-giving air. But even as he did, he knew that he had lost. He was hit—not once but twice. Even if he didn't drown, he would be swept helplessly along downstream for half a mile or more. He'd never get back in time.

His leg was numb. So was his left arm. But he found he could move both if he tried. He clenched his jaws and concentrated on staying afloat. He wondered how fast the water was running, how far away he would be when he managed to crawl out on dry land again.

Hail in the water had turned it icy. His good leg cramped. He suddenly felt panic.

There was no certainty that he'd get out of this alive. He might drown. He began to fight harder, and each time lightning flashed, he glanced around desperately, looking for something he could seize, looking for a spot along the precipitous banks where he could crawl out.

Either the water had dropped, he realized, or the wash had gotten deeper as he was swept along. The banks were perpendicular, and level ground was three feet above the surface of the water.

No chance to climb out. Unless. . . .

He saw it suddenly, a place where another wash entered

this one. The second wash was also filled with water, but it was still water, eddying and whirling and flecked with foam.

In a frantic burst of effort, he swam toward it, fighting the numbness in one arm and leg, the cramp in the other leg. He felt his head go under.

And then he was in the quiet water, and at last across it, and feeling the bottom of the wash beneath his feet. He staggered forward in running water that reached his knees. He collapsed against the side of the bank, half in the water, half out of it. His chest heaved like a bellows and he closed his eyes.

He must have lost consciousness because, when he opened his eyes again, the sky was gray with the coming dawn.

The rain had stopped. The wash in which he had so nearly drowned was empty now, empty save for a foot-wide trickle down the center of it.

The pain in both his arm and leg was excruciating. He stirred, grimaced, then struggled into an upright position by clawing up the muddy side of the wash. Leaving it, he staggered along the bottom, searching for a place sloping enough to allow him to crawl out.

He found one at last. He stopped, staring at it, wondering if he had enough strength left to make it out. Then determinedly he started up. He made it almost to the top before he lost his balance and rolled back down again. He lay still for a moment, raging at his own helplessness, cursing softly under his breath. His breath came in ragged gasps.

He stayed there until his breathing quieted. Then he crawled up a second time. This time he made it all the way to the top and poked his head over the rim before he lost his grip and rolled back again.

But he had seen something. He had seen a lone wagon approaching a quarter mile away.

He did not rest as long this time. He had to make it out onto level ground before the wagon got this far, or they'd pass by without seeing him.

There was fresh determination in him as he clawed his way up a third time. He got his arms over the edge and hung there precariously. The wagon came on until he could make out who was driving it.

Donna Cory. Alone. Soaked and bedraggled and muddy, but searching back and forth across the landscape with her eyes and calling out occasionally, "Vince! Vince!"

He stared blankly, using what remained of his strength to hold on, to stay where he was. His feet began to slip on the muddy bank below.

She was nearly to him, but she hadn't seen him yet.

He croaked, "Donna! Here! Over here!"

She heard him call and her eyes searched desperately. He felt his feet sliding, felt his arms slipping off the bank.

He yelled, "Here! Hurry!" and dug his fingers into the sod in an effort to hold on.

Her wagon halted instantly when she saw him. She jumped down, nearly fell, recovered, and ran toward him.

She caught his hands as they began to slide. She crouched, digging in her heels to hold him there.

He rested a moment, staring into her muddy face. Then he nodded.

She began to pull. At the same time, he wriggled upward. At last he flopped out onto level ground like a fish landed by an overly eager fisherman.

Donna was crying silently, staring at the blood that had soaked both his shoulder and his thigh. She gave him time to rest, then said, "Lean on me. I'll help you up. If we can get to the wagon—"

With her help, he made it up. Leaning heavily on her, he made it to the wagon and up over the endgate to lie unconscious just inside.

He had a vague recollection of the wagon's jolting motion. And then he knew no more.

chapter 17

When he regained consciousness, he was stripped and dry. He stirred, felt the pain of both wounds, and suddenly groped with his hands. Both wounds had been bandaged. There was a smell of whiskey in the wagon. He supposed it had been used to clean the wounds.

It was almost dark. He licked his lips and croaked, "Hey! Anybody around?"

The canvas parted at the rear of the wagon and he saw Donna's face. Her hair was dry and combed. There was no longer mud on her face, but it was thin and pale.

He said, "The wagons?"

"They're gone. Abel and Coulter took the gold wagons south. Mr. Effinger and the others headed east. I stayed to look for you."

"How long?"

"I found you this morning. It's evening now."

He was silent for a moment. Abel and Coulter already had a twenty-four-hour start. He'd never find them now. But that didn't mean he wouldn't try. He struggled into a sitting position. "My clothes."

"Not yet. You can't get up yet. You've lost an awful lot of blood."

His head reeled. He shook it angrily. "To hell with that. Get my clothes."

She studied his face briefly. Then, silently, she withdrew. She returned a moment later and handed him his clothes, which had been washed and dried. "Do you need some help?"

"Well—"

Her face flushed. She climbed up into the wagon and stripped the blankets back.

103

There was no struggling with her. Firmly, she pulled his underwear on over his feet and met his eyes mockingly as he yanked it up to cover him. She murmured, "You didn't think I would, did you?"

He grunted and reached for his pants. Again she helped him get them over his feet. But he pulled them up himself.

Weakness rolled over him in waves. The mocking expression left Donna's eyes. "You shouldn't——"

"If you think I'm going to let those two get away with five million dollars in gold, then you're not thinking straight. I—" His voice trailed off.

She said, "You stay here. They left me some dried venison and I've made some soup."

She climbed out of the wagon. MacIvers put on his shirt, slowly and carefully. Maybe he couldn't ride a horse, or even a mule. But he could lie here in the wagon while it followed the trail of the gold wagons south.

Donna returned and handed him a bowl of soup. He put his back against one of the wagon bows and spooned it into his mouth. It was scalding and delicious, but it stirred nausea in his stomach. He fought the nausea and finished it. He'd never regain his strength if he didn't eat.

He said, "Tomorrow——"

"Tomorrow we can head south, if you insist on it. Tonight you rest."

He nodded wearily, waited a moment, then said with some surprise, "You'll help? I thought—"

She met his glance briefly, then looked away. "Perhaps a woman's principles are not as strong as those of a man. Maybe my beliefs were more my husband's beliefs than my own. Now—" Her eyes sparkled defiantly. "I wouldn't leave a dog out here to die alone. I'd help him get where he wanted to go if only because I felt sorry for him."

He felt drowsiness coming over him, but he summoned the strength to ask, "Is the trail rained out? Or can we follow it?"

"It's plain enough. Those wagons were heavy. Their wheels sank several inches into the mud."

He nodded weakly and closed his eyes. Donna took the bowl from his hands and climbed down out of the wagon. He heard her moving around outside.

He forced his mind to function and tried to guess where Abel and Coulter would go. They were headed south. They didn't dare turn east because by the time they reached the settlements Effinger would have alerted the authorities.

They might turn east into Arkansas. But it was far more likely that they'd continue south. Across Cherokee country into Texas and beyond. But they'd probably cache most of the gold somewhere along the way.

His chances of catching up with them were slim, he realized. They would be two nights and a day ahead of him, but as long as the trail held out—and even after that—he'd go on. He'd find them eventually, even if he didn't find the gold.

He slept, sometimes deeply and restfully, sometimes lightly, troubled by meaningless dreams. He was back in Texas on his ranch. Comanches were riding in, painted, howling, firing guns and arrows, and rushing toward the house with flaming torches. Helen was there in the house with him, but her face was like Donna Cory's face.

He awoke with a start. He was soaked with sweat. The sun was sending a shaft of light through a small tear in the canvas top.

He could hear Donna moving around outside. After what seemed a long time she appeared at the rear of the wagon with another bowl of soup and some fresh-baked biscuits.

He was hungry this morning. He finished eating quickly. She said, "The mules are harnessed. I guess we're ready to go."

He nodded and handed his bowl to her. She studied his face for a moment. "You look better this morning. It's lucky both bullets went on through. Otherwise—"

She disappeared. He reached for his boots. They were stiff from the soaking they'd had, but they were dry. He pulled them on over his bare feet. Then he eased himself forward and climbed out on the wagon seat.

His head reeled and he gripped the seat for support. Donna climbed up and picked up the reins. She started to protest his being here, but the protest died as she glanced at his face.

His horse lay bloating a dozen yards away. The mules moved out, heading straight south along the plain trail left by the heavily loaded gold wagons. Looking around, MacIvers could see the trail left by the others as they headed east.

He stayed on the seat for almost an hour, swaying, fighting both the pain in his thigh and shoulder and the lightness in his head. At last he could stay erect no longer. He motioned for her to halt and crawled weakly back to his blankets in the wagon bed. He fell asleep almost instantly and did not awake again until it was dark.

But he felt stronger tonight then he had this morning. And he would be stronger tomorrow than he had been today.

He ate, slept again, and awoke this time as dawn was beginning to gray the sky.

The trail ran undeviatingly south, no longer as plain as it had been before because the gold wagons no longer traveled in mud. But it was plain enough.

MacIvers kept a careful eye on the horizons all around. Effinger would have reached the settlements by now. He would have alerted the authorities. MacIvers knew he could expect interception at any time.

He saw the lone rider while he was still several miles away. He watched the man approach.

A single rider. Coming hard from the north. Following the same trail MacIvers was following. Or MacIvers' trail.

The man was still a quarter mile away when MacIvers recognized him. It was John Busby, riding a horse MacIvers had never seen before.

John pulled up beside the wagon. Donna halted it. For an instant John was speechless. At last he said, "I'm glad to see you, Mr. MacIvers. I—we all thought you were dead. But when I'd had time to think about it—well, I just didn't know. Nobody'd actually seen you. And anyway, it didn't seem possible. I was going to enlist as soon as we got home, but I figured maybe it'd be better if I just came on back." He grinned. "Now I'm glad I did."

"So am I."

"You think you'll catch up with them?"

MacIvers shrugged, then winced with the sudden stab of pain. "What about Effinger? Has he contacted anyone?"

Busby nodded, his face worried now. "They said there was a telegraph station in the next town. So the town marshal went himself, with Mr. Effinger. They sent a message to some Union garrison. I expect the troopers are on the way. That was another reason I came back."

MacIvers glanced at John's saddle horse. If Union troops intercepted them, chances were they'd arrest him. He said, "I'm going to take your horse, John."

"Sure, Mr. MacIvers." John started to dismount.

Donna protested, "You can't! With all that jolting, why, you wouldn't get ten miles away."

"Maybe not. But I'm going to try." He climbed carefully down from the wagon seat. When he reached the ground, he was bathed with sweat. John looked at him worriedly, but handed him the reins anyway.

MacIvers tried to mount, but he couldn't raise his wounded leg far enough to get his foot into the stirrup. He glared at John. "Damn it, give me a boost!"

Donna said quietly, "Before you do, take a look back there. Do you think you can outrun them?"

106

Irritably MacIvers turned his head.

There must have been twenty of them, coming on at a steady trot. Union troopers, blue-clad, in a column of twos. At their head rode an officer and a guidon bearer.

MacIvers leaned helplessly against the wagon wheel. She was right. He couldn't outrun them. Trying would be foolish and would weaken him even more.

Silently he watched the troop draw near. When they reached the wagon, they halted. Their officer, a lieutenant, approached. His expression was wary, his eyes cold. "Identify yourself, sir."

"MacIvers." MacIvers gestured toward Donna with his head. "Mrs. Cory. And John Busby."

"Anyone else?"

MacIvers shook his head.

"We'll have to search your wagon." The lieutenant's eyes glanced ahead of the wagon at the trail of the other two.

MacIvers shrugged. "Go ahead and search."

The lieutenant barked an order at his men. Three of them approached, dismounted, and climbed into the wagon bed. After several minutes they climbed out again. "Nothin' there, sir."

The lieutenant looked coldly at MacIvers. "You're under arrest. Mr. MacIvers. For treason. You will accompany us."

Donna said, "He will *not* accompany you, lieutenant. Unless you want to arrive wherever you're going with a dead man on your hands. He's wounded. You can see that. He can't even get on a horse."

The lieutenant studied MacIvers for a moment. He glanced at Donna's face. He nodded with a brief, cold smile and touched his hat brim with his hand. "Perhaps you're right, ma'am. But he is still under arrest. I'll leave a trooper as a guard. You will proceed straight south. I will leave a marker west of Baxter Springs. You will turn east there."

Neither Donna nor MacIvers replied.

The lieutenant turned his head and barked, "Johansen. Get these people's guns. Then ride with this wagon. This man is under arrest."

A sandy-haired trooper about twenty-five detached himself from the others. He took MacIvers' revolver and John Busby's rifle and handed them up to one of the troopers. The lieutenant raised a hand, and the troop thundered away.

MacIvers climbed resignedly to the wagon seat. Things were steadily getting worse, he thought ruefully. He hadn't a chance of catching the gold wagons now. Not before the lieutenant did.

The gold was lost. It was only a matter of time before it would be in Union hands.

Then his jaw hardened and his eyes narrowed angrily. Donna glanced at his face and slapped the mules' backs with the reins. The wagon rolled ponderously ahead once more.

The gold wasn't lost, MacIvers thought grimly, until it actually was in Union hands. Until then. . . .

All that day they creaked steadily south. And the following day, and the day after that. There was a new closeness between MacIvers and Donna, a closeness that needed no expression in words. John Busby usually rode along behind the wagon at the trooper's side.

MacIvers could feel his strength returning with each day that passed. Johansen, the trooper, began to watch him more carefully.

On the fifth day after their interception by the cavalry, they halted at a spot where the wagon trail turned east. Here, also, they found the marker the lieutenant had left for them, a bandanna tied to a scrubby bush.

MacIvers climbed down from the wagon and walked slowly back and forth, reading the tracks in the ground.

It was very plain what had happened here. This was the place the lieutenant had caught up with Abel and Coulter.

They had not surrendered easily. There had been a running battle, with the wagons yanked along by running mules, the cavalry thundering along beside the two. Walking on, he found the place where either Coulter or Abel had tumbled from the wagon seat. There was a spot of blood on the ground half as big as a man's hat. Nearby lay a dead and bloating mule.

Farther on he found where the other driver had pulled up. There was blood here too, where he had apparently stood on the ground and surrendered to them.

He returned to the wagon slowly and thoughtfully. He climbed up to the seat, feigning more difficulty than he experienced. Donna drove on, eastward now, occasionally glancing worriedly at his face.

A mile farther on, he saw a man's hat lying on the ground. He recognized it as Abel's hat.

Donna said, "They've got the gold. And Abel and Coulter are dead. Aren't they?"

He nodded. "One's dead, that's sure. The other probably is too. If he's not, he soon will be."

"What are you going to do?"

"Tonight I'm going to take Johansen's horse. I'm going on ahead."

"What good will that do? You can't take the gold away from that troop of cavalry. You can't take on the whole Union army by yourself."

He grinned at her humorlessly. "Maybe I won't have to do it all by myself. That's what I mean to find out."

chapter 18

At dusk MacIvers halted the wagon. John Busby dismounted immediately and began to unhitch the mules. Johansen sat his horse nearby, watching MacIvers warily.

MacIvers let Donna climb down first and accepted her help in getting down himself. He looked at Johansen irritably. "Trooper, if we're going to have a fire, we're going to need some wood."

The trooper looked at John Busby, busily unharnessing the mules. He glanced back at MacIvers.

Reluctantly he dismounted. He glanced at MacIvers again, then tied his horse to one of the wagon wheels, and walked away into the gathering darkness.

MacIvers looked down into Donna's face. "You'll be all right. The trooper will see to it that you get safely to Baxter Springs."

"Will I see you again?"

He nodded. "Wait in Baxter Springs for me. I'll find you."

He wished he could see her face more clearly. In the almost complete darkness it was only a blur. Suddenly she reached up with both her hands. She pulled his head down and kissed him on the mouth. She murmured, "I'll be there, Vince. I'll wait for you."

She stepped back, and he untied Johansen's horse. He mounted awkwardly and with difficulty, wincing as he put weight on his wounded leg. He settled himself in the saddle and smiled down at her, aware that his face was bathed with sweat.

Her voice was soft, "Be careful."

He nodded, turned the horse, and walked the animal slowly away. He rode this way for nearly a quarter mile.

Then he urged the horse into a rolling lope, his face turning white with the sharp stabbing pains caused by the movement under him.

Johansen might try pursuing him on John Busby's horse, but he couldn't trail at night. By morning MacIvers would be in Baxter Springs.

A mile fell behind. Suddenly he caught the distant beat of hoofs behind him. Coming on fast, they made a dull thunder in the air.

He halted, knowing the trooper would pass him in the dark. He leaned forward and put a hand over the horse's nostrils so that the animal wouldn't give him away.

He removed the hand immediately when he heard John Busby's yell, "Mr. MacIvers! Mr. MacIvers! Where are you?"

He called, "Over here," and waited until John reached him and pulled up his plunging horse. John said, "I'm goin' with you, Mr. MacIvers. Mrs. Cory said I was to catch you and look out for you."

MacIvers shrugged, too weak to argue with the boy. He touched the trooper's horse with his heels, and the animal moved on, walking first, then breaking into a lope again. MacIvers clung to the saddle with both hands. His head felt light, and dizziness rolled over him in waves.

What did he expect to accomplish, he wondered gloomily. He was too weak to fight, and he didn't have a gun. The Union army had the gold, and he could bet it would be well guarded, at least until it was deep in Union territory.

As though voicing his own doubts, John yelled, "What are you going to do, Mr. MacIvers? What can you do?"

MacIvers frowned. "Find out where it is. Then see if I can get help."

Help. From Southern forces in Arkansas if he could get there in time. Or from irregulars—the raiders who had burned Lawrence the year before, who had attacked Blunt's command at Baxter Springs the same year.

He refused himself the luxury of admitting the difficulty. He had but one course left.

But as the hours passed, hope of success faded with his waning strength. When he halted outside Baxter Springs at dawn, he could scarcely stay on his horse. He knew that if he dismounted, he would never get on again.

He stared at the sleeping town, then turned and glanced at John Busby's face. He said hoarsely, "I'm going to need some help."

Busby jumped off his horse and helped him to dismount. MacIvers sank weakly to the ground, hidden by high

111

grass from the land surrounding them. "I've got to know where that gold is, and I can't go in myself. You wanted to enlist. Well, now's your chance."

Busby's eyes were scared, but his jaw was firm. "I'll go, Mr. MacIvers."

MacIvers nodded. "Then tie the horses over in that grove of trees. Leave me right here. Go in on foot and find out what you can."

"Yes, sir." The boy saluted awkwardly. He picked up the reins of the two horses and led them away toward the grove of trees. He returned a few moments later. He seemed about to speak, but changed his mind. He hurried away toward the town.

MacIvers closed his eyes. The earth beneath him seemed to be whirling. He felt his consciousness slip.

He slept, and the sun mounted in the sky until it reached a point from which it beat directly into his face. He awoke, sweating, his mouth dry and cottony.

For several moments he lay still. Then he forced himself up to his knees. He could now peer over the top of the tall grass. He could see the town.

There were people walking in the streets. And he saw John Busby walking toward him across the open plain.

He sank back and closed his eyes. After what seemed a long, long time, Busby reached him. "I located it, Mr. MacIvers. It's in a livery stable on the far edge of town. There are two troopers on guard in front and two in back. I'd know the wheel tracks of those wagons anywhere and I saw them heading into that livery barn. Anyhow, I don't reckon they'd be guarding it unless there was something inside to guard."

He squatted beside MacIvers, who saw that he was carrying a gunnysack. He dumped it out on the ground. "I got some bread. And I stole some apples off a tree."

MacIvers forced himself up to one elbow. He took some of the bread and forced it down. He followed it with an apple, which eased his thirst somewhat. He said, "We'll stay here until dark. Are the horses out of sight?"

"Yes, sir. I tied 'em in a real thick bunch of trees. You'd never see 'em unless you was right on top of 'em."

MacIvers sank back and closed his eyes again. He didn't know the terrain that lay ahead of him. And he wasn't sure he would be believed, even if he did succeed in contacting some unit of the Army of the Confederacy. A tale of stolen gold, it was not the most believable yarn in the world. If there was red tape or delay, the gold would be gone by the time he got back to Baxter Springs.

He slept again. At dusk he was wakened by Busby, gently

shaking him by the arm. "Mr. MacIvers. It's gettin' dark."

He roused himself with difficulty. The pain in shoulder and thigh was like fire, continuous and unrelenting. He croaked, "Get the horses."

Busby left, and a few moments later came back, leading the horses. He boosted MacIvers to the saddle. MacIvers sat there swaying dizzily.

He stared at the town for a moment, at the lights beginning to wink in the houses and stores. Then he led out, circling the town and heading south.

He rode at a steady walk, hunched in his saddle in such a way that neither shoulder nor leg was jolted more than necessary. Last night, he knew, both wounds had bled considerably. Tonight they would bleed some more. And with the blood that seeped out of them and soaked the bandages went his strength.

Again tonight he clung to the saddle with both hands. And the hours slowly passed.

He didn't know when they crossed the border into Arkansas. But as morning began to dawn, he saw the broken hills ahead.

He halted at the first farmhouse he saw. He rode up to the door and stared weakly at the bearded man and at the woman, her brood of children peeping from behind her skirts. "This Arkansas, mister?" he asked.

The man nodded without speaking. His eyes rested steadily on the hip of MacIvers' horse. MacIvers realized suddenly that the Union army brand, U.S., was plainly visible. He said, "Where's the nearest army detachment?"

The man's expression became sullenly suspicious.

MacIvers said irritably, "All right, so you think I'm a spy. Don't tell me then. But I have information that is of tremendous value to the Confederacy. Get on one of these horses and find someone to tell that to. Bring 'em back here. Tell them I need at least fifty men for a raid."

The man turned around and picked up an ancient rifle from beside the door. He came out and stood at the head of John Busby's horse while John swung down. Without a word he mounted, drummed on the horse's ribs with his bare heels, and rode away, heading up into the hills.

John helped MacIvers dismount. They crossed the yard, and MacIvers sank down in the shade of a cottonwood. After several moments the woman brought out two bowls of stew and two cups of warm milk.

MacIvers ate as much as he could and drank the milk. Then he put his back against the tree trunk and closed his eyes.

He slept and did not wake until late afternoon.

John Busby was shaking his unhurt arm. "Mr. MacIvers! Here they come!"

He opened his eyes. He saw them pouring in through the gate, but there weren't fifty of them. There were only fifteen.

They wore no uniforms. Some were bearded; some were not. They ranged in age from about fourteen to sixty. But they had one thing in common. All were heavily armed. Some had two pistols thrust into their belts. Most wore cartridge belts, slung diagonally across their chests. About half of them carried rifles in their hands.

The farmer was with them. He pointed silently at the pair beneath the cottonwood.

The raiders spread until they surrounded the tree. One of them dismounted and approached.

Busby stood up and saluted. MacIvers stayed where he was.

The raider was well over six feet tall and must have weighed two hundred pounds. His eyes were a light, tawny brown, his hair beginning to turn gray. He said, "Who are you, mister, and what are you doing here?"

"MacIvers. Captain, Virginia Volunteers." He began his story, telling of his solitary journey to California and of the wagon-train journey east carrying the gold. He ended with the location of the gold wagons in Baxter Springs. He gave the man the name of his colonel and his regiment so that his story could be verified by telegraph.

The men stared down at him suspiciously. "The telegraph wires are down, but maybe you knew that all along. What am I supposed to do, swallow this crazy tale and take my men into Baxter Springs?"

"Five million dollars will buy a lot of guns."

"Maybe. And maybe forty or fifty Union troopers are waiting there for us. They'd like to get their hands on us."

MacIvers stared steadily at him. "I've told you all I can. There were twenty men in the troop that captured the gold. Maybe there are more, and maybe there aren't."

"If we go, you go along. If it's a trap, you'll be the first to die."

MacIvers nodded. "I expected to go along."

"All right then." He turned and bawled an order. A man approached leading a horse. Busby helped MacIvers mount. Then he swung to the back of MacIvers' horse.

The guerrilla commander said, "If we start now, we'll get there about two o'clock. I'm Justin Smith."

He led out, MacIvers and Busby following. Behind them came the guerrilla band.

The sun sank into the plain ahead of them. Dusk crept

softly across the land. At last the sky was completely dark.

Fifteen men. Seventeen, counting Busby and himself. And while the advantage of surprise would be with them, they still weren't going to find it easy, taking on a town the size of Baxter Springs.

Furthermore, there was the problem of getting the two heavily loaded wagons safely back to Arkansas and hidden in the hills where the pursuing cavalry couldn't find them. Someone was going to have to fight a rearguard action. Someone was going to have to stop pursuit long enough for the ponderous wagons to get away.

But he was a little stronger tonight than he had been earlier. His head felt steadier. Pain did not trouble him as much. Besides, this war was more to his liking than the war of deception he had fought all the way from California. This was a war fought in the open.

Justin Smith ranged his horse alongside of MacIvers' horse. He handed a heavy revolver across the intervening space. "You'll need this."

MacIvers took it and thrust it into his belt. At last the column halted in sight of Baxter Springs.

MacIvers asked, "What's the plan?"

"Hell, we'll just ride in. We'll kill the guards and drive the wagons out. We'll leave about eight men to hold back pursuit, and we'll get the wagons away."

MacIvers shook his head. "They've got too many men for that. I told you there were at least twenty in that troop of cavalry. And there are the men in town."

"You got a better idea, cap'n?"

MacIvers nodded. "You need a diversion to pull the troops over to the other edge of town. You need something to keep them and the townsmen from cutting you to bits."

"Like what?"

"Fire. Send a couple of your men to set fire to some buildings on the far side of town. Give the fires time to get going good, and give the cavalry and the townspeople time to get over there and get busy fighting it. Then hit the livery barn. Do it with as little shooting as possible. Could be you'd get the wagons without anybody knowing it."

The man nodded. He turned his head. "Shanks, you and Dunham circle the town and come in from the other side. Fire the loft in Pelucci's Livery Stable. Go down that alley behind it and fire five or six of those private stables. They've all got hay in 'em; it shouldn't take you long. Then ride out and come back here."

The two separated themselves from the others and started away into the darkness.

Smith called softly, "And don't get caught."

It was the waiting now, waiting and watching for the fires that soon would start. MacIvers guessed it was after two o'clock. A few dogs barked, faintly heard at this distance. A breeze stirred and freshened, blowing from the north. Blowing from the prairie toward the town. It would blow the flames across the town, igniting other buildings in their path.

Nearly half an hour passed. And then, at last, MacIvers saw a tongue of flame on the far edge of the town. He watched it closely. Tension was building in him, driving away his weakness and much of his pain.

The fire leaped higher from the livery-stable roof. It illuminated other buildings nearby. It illuminated running figures that suddenly appeared in the streets.

A bell began to ring, a bell that sounded like one in the town church. Other bells added their clanging to the first. A fire engine, drawn by four horses, raced toward the scene of the fire, bell clanging noisily.

Other fires now appeared, growing from smaller buildings near the burning livery stable. And more running figures gathered to fight the flames.

Shanks and Dunham joined the group silently.

Justin Smith asked, "Anybody see you?"

"We were out of there before anybody stirred."

Smith looked at MacIvers questioningly.

MacIvers said, "All right, let's go. But walk the horses in. And don't shoot unless there's no other way."

They moved out silently, approaching the dark buildings on this side of town. Even if they were forced to shoot, thought MacIvers, it wasn't going to matter much. The bells were still pealing inside the town. Everyone was shouting. There was the fire engine's noise. It was doubtful that the shots would be heard.

He wished, suddenly, that Shanks and Dunham had set only one fire instead of five or six. The lieutenant wasn't a fool. If it occurred to him that the fires had been set. . . .

But it was too late to worry about that now. Whatever happened, there would never be another opportunity to recover the gold for the Confederacy.

chapter 19

At the first building they reached, Smith raised a hand. The column halted. Ahead, MacIvers could see the livery-barn roof, towering above the intervening smaller buildings.

Smith turned his head. "The fire was a good idea. What's next?"

"Take half your men and circle around behind the livery barn. I'll take the rest and come up on it from the front. I'll wait two or three minutes to give you time to get into position."

The man nodded and started away. About half his men followed him. The group disappeared into the darkness.

It had sounded so easy, thought MacIvers, but he had a feeling it wasn't going to be that easy. He remembered the face of the lieutenant. That one wasn't going to be fooled long by a diversion such as the fires on the other side of town. The minute he realized they had been set on purpose. . . .

He waited a moment more, then said softly, "Come on," and rode down the center of the dark street, the guerrillas fanning out behind.

Busby stayed close, watching him anxiously. Once he said, "You feel all right. Mr. MacIvers?"

"I'm all right."

The pain was constant in his shoulder and thigh, but it was bearable. And he was able to sit upright in the saddle without holding on. An hour, he thought, if he could hold on for one more hour.

He rounded a corner and saw the bulk of the livery barn. He saw the two dark shapes, one on each side of the wide door.

From behind the building he suddenly heard two shots. The guards stiffened and their carbines came up.

117

MacIvers raised his revolver. He thumbed the hammer back, sighted as carefully as possible in darkness, and fired. One of the guards, the one on the right, slammed against the building wall, then collapsed at its foot. The other whirled and fired blindly.

Behind MacIvers, several guns roared simultaneously. The second guard folded silently to the ground.

He turned his head and shouted, "Get inside! Put eight mules on each wagon. Two or three of you stay out here."

He rode swiftly to the livery-stable door. One of the men had dismounted. Busby dismounted to help him. The man said, "There's a padlock on the door."

"Shoot it off."

The man's gun blasted. The bullet clanged against the lock. A moment later the door swung open. Four of the guerrillas disappeared inside.

MacIvers rode to the door and stared inside. Dimly he could see the two wagons, facing his way. Dimly, beyond, he could see the open rear door, the corral, and the men out there.

It would take at least twenty minutes to catch mules, harness them, and hitch them to the wagons. He turned his head. "Keep a sharp lookout. This is going to take a little time."

There was confusion in the corral beyond the barn as the men out there began to catch the mules. There was noise. Too many guns had been fired. MacIvers knew how well the sound of a gun carries, particularly at night. The shots could have been heard on the far side of town despite the noise of bells and the crackling of the flames. The cavalry patrol might be forming even now. If they were, they'd be coming before the wagons could get away. On foot perhaps. It was doubtful if they had their horses at this time of night. But they'd be even more formidable on foot than they would be mounted.

Time dragged. He strained his eyes into the darkness beyond the livery barn until he began to see moving shapes that weren't even there. His horse fidgeted, but he held him still with a harsh hand on the reins.

He could hear the rattle of harness rings inside, the stamping of the restless mules, and occasionally a man's soft curse. They were working fast, but they were hampered by darkness. At last he heard the clank of tugs and the banging of single-trees. It was almost done.

His eye caught a running form a hundred yards up the street. It materialized, and behind it came other forms. He yelled, "Here they come! All of you that can, get on out here!"

118

Running feet inside the barn. Those outside swung from their horses' backs and hurriedly led the uneasy animals into the barn.

MacIvers stayed in his saddle, knowing the difficulty he would have remounting. He made a good target on his horse, but he didn't dare dismount.

Carbines rattled in the street. Bullets tore into the flimsy walls of the livery barn. A horse uttered a shrill sound as he was hit. From inside the barn, from the shadow of the walls outside, the guerrillas opened fire.

No longer could MacIvers see the running forms of the cavalrymen. They had sought shelter in doorways and behind buildings. But he could see the flashes of their carbines.

He turned his horse and rode through the door into the livery barn. He rode to the first wagon. "Is it ready?"

"Ready to go, cap'n. Any time you say."

He rode on to the second. It was also ready to go. He called, "John! John Busby!"

The boy came running.

MacIvers said, "Get up on the seat of this one here. Wait till I give you the word. Then drive like hell."

He rode on through the barn and out the wide rear door. It opened directly into the corral, which still held thirty or forty horses and mules. If the wagons could be turned, if they could get out this way. . . .

His horse's hoofs sank in the soft ground just outside the door, ground that had been softened by overflow from a water trough nearby. He rode on across the corral. There was a gate and a narrow road beyond.

He returned and halted immediately before the door. It was too soft here, he thought, for the weight the wagons were carrying. Each held four tons of gold. If one of them bogged down. . . .

Helplessly he stared at the horses and mules milling on the far side of the corral. He crossed the corral again and looked at the horses, crowded in a corner against the fence. All of them were big. All were dark in color. Army horses, he thought triumphantly.

He rode back into the stable, feeling less helpless now. Firing outside had dwindled to a spasmodic crackle because of the lack of clear targets for both sides.

The minute the wagons rolled out, all the cavalrymen would have to do would be to shoot the mules. And even though there was no light right now, sooner or later the lieutenant was sure to realize what an advantage light would give to him. He'd set fire to a nearby building to obtain it. The guerrillas and the gold wagons would be trapped inside the livery barn.

He needed a diversion, and he needed it immediately. But he had the means to create one now.

He yelled, "A couple of you mount up and get out in back. Push those horses and mules straight through the stable. We're going to drive 'em up the street."

Two or three men mounted and rode past the wagons and out the wide rear door.

MacIvers said, more softly now, "I want about six more. Go out the front door and split, three to the right, three to the left. Circle around and position yourselves in that street behind the troop of cavalry. We've got their horses out back in the corral. We're going to drive 'em up the street. They'll forget about the wagons for a few minutes when they see their horses getting away. But I don't want a single horse to get through. I want every damn one of 'em shot." He waited a moment, then went on, "As soon as it's done, circle back and cover the wagons in the rear."

"How'll you know when we're in position?"

"Fire three shots. Three quick ones."

The six grouped before the door. Then, as though at a signal, they thundered through it into the darkness outside.

Immediately the guns of the cavalrymen opened up. One horse went down. But the other five disappeared, two turning right, the other three left.

MacIvers heard the horses and mules crowding into the barn behind him. He put his horse crossways in the doorway. A minute passed.

He listened intently for the signal which would tell him the five were in position behind the cavalrymen. Another minute passed, a third, a fourth.

And then he heard them, three shots fired from a revolver in quick succession. He moved his horse aside. He roared, "Drive 'em, and drive 'em fast!"

The first of the horses and mules streamed past. He fired his revolver and yelled.

The remaining guerrillas followed suit. Guns, roaring hollowly inside the barn, made a sudden, rumbling thunder. The terrified horses and mules broke into a frantic gallop and streamed out into the street.

The spasmodic firing of the cavalrymen halted immediately. MacIvers shouted, "All right, roll the wagons!"

Busby whipped up his teams. The first wagon rolled ponderously through the door.

MacIvers roared, "Faster! Whip 'em up!"

Busby's whip snaked out. The wagon picked up speed. The second wagon began to roll.

120

Busby's wagon made a sharp left turn, taking the road that led out of town. The other wagon began the turn.

The horses and mules were past the cavalrymen now. MacIvers saw their dim shapes emerge from concealment and run in the dusty wake of the galloping herd. Beyond, he saw the flashing of the guerrillas' guns as they began to slaughter the fleeing animals.

A roar of rage went up from the pursuing, frantically running cavalrymen. Their commander shouted an order for them to return, but it was lost in the noise of galloping hoofs, in the crackling of guerrilla guns, in the rumble of the two wagons as they picked up speed.

Their commander ran toward the livery stable alone. He halted and raised his gun.

MacIvers' gun and his sounded almost simultaneously. The man staggered forward a few steps, tripped on his saber, and sprawled in the dust. He began to crawl, but he did not fire a second time.

The second wagon lurched violently. Its driver tumbled from the seat and a wheel rolled over him.

MacIvers yanked his horse around so violently that the animal reared. He raced alongside the wagon. He slipped his feet from the stirrups and brought up his legs. Damn it, if the wounded leg gave out now. . . .

He got his feet against the saddle, straightened his legs, and drove his body upward, out toward the wagon seat. He felt his bad leg give; he clawed frantically for one of the wagon bows. He caught it, felt his body drag down between the wagon and the great front wheel. Then he was scrambling, clawing, pulling himself up toward the seat. He reached it, panting, weak from exertion and pain. His head whirled, and he could feel the warmth of new blood soaking his bandages. He clawed for the reins in the darkness, got a handful, and began frantically to sort them out. Busby's wagon was out of sight ahead of him. MacIvers' mules were hopelessly snarled.

He snatched the long whip and snapped it out toward the lead team. They lunged against the traces.

Order came slowly out of the tangle. But at last the wagon tongue straightened out and the teams began to pull.

Cavalrymen were now running back, firing as they ran. The remaining guerrillas formed a rear guard, firing steadily from their horses' backs, retreating as the wagon moved ahead of them.

Another two hundred yards, MacIvers thought. Another two hundred yards, and he'd be clear. There might be pursuit, but it would take awhile before it got organized.

But he was weakening. His thoughts began to grow hazy and his vision blurred. The shooting immediately behind the wagon seemed as though it was miles away. He fell sideways and banged his head on the forward wagon bow. He fought his way into an upright position. He had to have help, he realized. He was going to pass out, and he had to have someone to drive this wagon when he did. He opened his mouth to shout. But no sound came out. No sound except a hoarse croak that was lost in all the confusion and surrounding noise. He felt his head getting light again. He seemed to be floating. He gritted his teeth angrily. He blinked his eyes and shook his head. He clung to the reins like a drowning man might cling to a rope.

He thought he was dreaming. He heard someone screaming at him, screaming his name, and it sounded like a woman's voice.

He shook his head fiercely and stared ahead into the darkness. The lead team shied.

Something white was in the road. A woman. But that was impossible. The wagon drew abreast.

Plainly he heard her scream this time. "Vince! Vince! Stop for me!"

He hauled back on the reins. The wagon ground to a halt. Then she was climbing up, and he knew who it was. Donna. Donna Cory. Somehow she had gotten here; somehow she had understood when the fires started, when the guns began to sound, that MacIvers was behind it all.

She reached the seat and snatched the reins out of his hands. He fell against her and the world turned black.

He could not have been completely unconscious more than two or three minutes, but when he regained his senses, the guns were still.

The wagon rumbled along behind the four teams of trotting mules. Ahead, faintly, he could see the blur of white made by the canvas top of the wagon young Busby was driving.

He glanced behind and saw the glow in the sky caused by the fires still burning in the town. He turned his head and looked at Donna Cory's face.

He could not see clearly because of the darkness.

She asked, "How do you feel?"

"Better. How long have I been out?"

"Not long."

Several horsemen were trotting beside the wagon. One of them, whose voice he recognized as belonging to Justin Smith, yelled, "We got most of their horses, but we sure didn't get every horse in town. They'll be along."

"How many men have you got left?"

"Nine, counting myself."

Eleven, then, in all. It wasn't enough. It wasn't near enough. MacIvers yelled, "Can you send someone for more?"

"They wouldn't get back in time. They're more'n forty miles away."

MacIvers didn't reply to that. He clung to the seat and stared angrily into the darkness ahead. He was so tired, so weak, he couldn't seem to think. And he had to think. He had to come up with something, or everything they'd done so far would be wasted. If the wagons were recaptured, they would be lost for good.

chapter 20

For a long time MacIvers rode the jolting wagon seat in silence. Beside him, Donna Cory drove, occasionally glancing at him.

It seemed ridiculous to MacIvers that the battle to be fought soon might possibly be one of the most decisive of the war, yet it would be fought by less than thirty men. If the Union forces managed to recapture the wagons, and by so doing, deprived the Confederacy of the gold, it would be a major victory. If, on the other hand, they failed to recapture the gold, the war would at least be prolonged because of it.

He thought of the miles that lay behind, of the Sierras, of the desert, of the endless days and nights. His eyes narrowed with anger. There had to be a way. There *had* to be.

Eleven men. He yelled, "Drop off two men! Tell 'em to hold the road as long as they can."

He heard Smith call out two names. Two men fell back and disappeared.

The two could give them only a momentary respite, MacIvers realized. Another half hour at best.

The mules were tiring rapidly. It was hard for Donna to keep them at a trot. MacIvers took the whip from her and cracked it over the lead team's heads.

Ten minutes passed. Fifteen. MacIvers heard nothing from behind. He supposed they were beyond hearing range now. He yelled, "Drop off two more."

Four men sacrificed. He hoped the four, shooting from ambush, would reduce the odds before they were killed themselves.

He turned his head and stared toward the east. A line of gray was visible along the horizon. Dawn was coming. In another half hour it would be light enough to see the road. Fifteen minutes after that, it would be light enough to see for miles across the plain.

His plan of dropping off men to slow the pursuit would be useless in daylight. The pursuit would simply go around them and come on.

Slowly the light increased. At last, MacIvers heard the faint popping of gunfire from behind.

The second pair, he thought. He listened intently. When the gunfire stopped, it would be time to halt and make a stand.

He counted almost thirty shots. And then, suddenly, all was quiet again.

He could see the road now. He could see almost a hundred yards away from it. He turned his head and looked at the men riding beside the wagon.

Justin Smith had a cloth tied around his forearm. There was blood on the side of his face and neck from a bullet-pierced ear. One of the others carried his left arm awkwardly, blood dripping slowly from his fingertips.

Donna Cory's face was white with weariness.

MacIvers yelled, "Tell Busby to stop! We'll fight 'em off from here."

One of the guerrillas spurred alongside young Busby's wagon. It halted immediately. MacIvers pulled his wagon up close and halted it. He lifted his revolver from its holster and began reloading it.

The guerrillas dismounted, tied their horses to the wagon wheels, and climbed stiffly into the wagons. MacIvers finished reloading and stood up to peer over the canvas wagon top.

He could see them coming now. But there were only eight. Five wore the dark-blue uniforms of the cavalry. The other three were civilians.

He felt a surge of hope. Their casualties must have been heavier than he had dared to hope.

Donna Cory was looking steadily into his face. Her face was white, but her mouth was firm. She thought this was the end, he realized. The end for all of them. She said softly, "Vince, I want a gun."

"Those are Union troops back there."

"Do you think I care? They're trying to kill us—you, me, these men who are only doing what they think is right."

He nodded and called, "Smith, have you got an extra gun?"

Smith passed a rifle to him from inside the wagon. MacIvers handed it to her and stood up again. The troopers were now less than a quarter mile away. He said, "Get inside the wagon. Quick!"

125

Donna scrambled into the wagon. He followed, knelt behind the wagon seat, and rested his revolver on it.

Those in the rear of the wagon opened fire. A horseman thundered around the wagon, into MacIvers' view.

He steadied the revolver and thumbed the hammer back. He fired. Beside him, Donna's rifle roared almost simultaneously.

The trooper slumped over the horse's neck, hanging on with both arms. The horse swerved. The trooper was dumped from the saddle, but one boot hung in a stirrup. He was dragged for nearly a hundred yards before the boot came free. He lay still, crumpled awkwardly on the ground.

MacIvers heard Donna gasp. But he had no time to look at her. Two riders in civilian clothes came into sight, leaning forward in their saddles and firing as they rode.

MacIvers steadied the revolver again, but before he could fire, the man in the lead straightened and fell backward over his horse's rump. MacIvers quickly changed his point of aim and fired at the second one in line. His bullet struck the horse's neck, and the animal pitched forward, then somersaulted, throwing his rider clear. The man got up and began to run, straightaway from the wagons and into the empty plain.

The firing stopped as quickly as it had begun. MacIvers struggled out from beneath the canvas and stood up on the wagon seat. Three of the cavalrymen and one civilian lay dead on the ground. The others had withdrawn beyond the range of the guerrillas' guns. They were talking among themselves, apparently trying to decide what to do.

A poorly planned, poorly executed attack, thought MacIvers. If their commander had been with them, it might have turned out differently.

Only two troopers remained, and two civilians. Obviously the heart for the attack had been taken out of them. The civilian whose horse had been killed climbed up behind the other one. The four rode back toward town.

Smith climbed out onto the seat and picked up the reins. He said, "Get back into the wagon and stretch out. We'll take it from here."

Wearily, MacIvers crawled back into the wagon. Donna spread blankets for him. He closed his eyes, feeling her cool hand on his forehead.

There were hills, and narrow, rocky roads, and streams to ford. But the wagons ground along steadily, the remnants of the guerrilla band plodding along behind.

At last there was a town, and a ragged detachment of

Confederate regulars, and the gold being loaded onto a railroad car with a ten-man guard.

After that there was a house, a bed with clean white sheets, and excruciating pain as the local doctor cleaned and rebandaged MacIvers' wounds. He was unconscious for two days. Or at least partly so. But he did seem to be aware of someone always beside him whenever he stirred or made a sound.

It was early October. He opened his eyes, fully conscious at last, and saw that the person beside him was Donna, thin and tired, but smiling happily.

In mid-October he was able to get out of bed for the first time. He healed quickly after that. By early November all that was left of his wounds was their stiffness and a couple of angry scars.

He would go back soon. That knowledge showed itself in Donna's worried eyes. But for now they roamed the hills, flaming with autumn colors, and felt the raw bite of the wind, and lifted their faces to the chilling rain.

The war raged on, though it was evident to them both that the Confederacy was dying a little more with each day that passed. The gold had come too late.

The day came, as both had known it must, when MacIvers put on a Confederate uniform again and walked to the station as the train noisily approached the town.

Donna walked beside him, unusually silent.

He turned and faced her on the weathered station platform. He put out his arms and held her close.

He suddenly realized that his guilt was gone. He had done only what he'd thought was right. His failure to change the course of the war in no way altered that.

And with the realization came a sudden feeling of freedom he had not felt before. He said, "Will you wait until I come back?"

She nodded wordlessly.

He said, "You'll like Texas."

"If you're there, I will."

The train whistled insistently. It began to move. He bent his head and kissed her on the mouth. When he drew away, tears filled her eyes. He caught the handrail and swung onto the train.

Standing on the steps, he stared back at her. She stood very straight, a hand raised to shield her eyes from the sun. At this distance he could not see her tears, but he knew that they were there.

He had a feeling that when he returned, she would be

standing there, waiting, looking exactly as she looked now. He turned and climbed the steps into the railroad car. And he was smiling as he thought of all the good years that lay ahead.

THE END